Silas Marner

George Eliot

Level 3

Retold by A. J. Brayley

Series Editors: Andy Hopkins and Jocelyn Potter

Pearson Education Limited

Edinburgh Gate, Harlow,
Essex CM20 2JE, England
and Associated Companies throughout the world.

ISBN: 978-1-4082-0953-0

First published in the Longman Structural Readers Series 1968
Adapted for the Longman Fiction Series 1996
First Penguin Readers edition published 1999
This edition published 2009

1 3 5 7 9 10 8 6 4 2

Set in 11/13pt A. Garamond
Printed in China
SWTC/01

Produced for the Publishers by AC Estudio Editorial S.L.

Published by Pearson Education Ltd in association with Penguin Books Ltd,
both companies being subsidiaries of Pearson Plc

Acknowledgements

We are grateful to the following for permission to reproduce photographs:

(Key: b-bottom; c-centre; l-left; r-right; t-top)

Getty Images: WireImage / John Shearer 75l; WireImage / Steve Granitz 75r;
PA Photos: AP / John McConnico 75c; **Rex Features:** Sipa Press 74

Every effort has been made to trace the copyright holders and we apologise in advance
for any unintentional omissions. We would be pleased to insert the appropriate
acknowledgement in any subsequent edition of this publication.

For a complete list of the titles available in the Penguin Active Reading series please write to your local
Pearson Longman office or to: Penguin Readers Marketing Department, Pearson Education,
Edinburgh Gate, Harlow, Essex CM20 2JE, England.

Contents

1.1 What's the book about?

Read the title of Chapter 1 and the new words at the bottom of page 1. Look at the picture on the same page. Then talk to another student and answer these questions. What do you think?

1 Does this story happen in the present or the past? ....

2 What is Silas Marner's job? ....

3 How old is Silas Marner? ....

4 Is the man next to Silas a friend or an enemy? ....

5 Are these two men rich? ....

6 Is Raveloe a place or a person? ....

1.2 What happens first?

1 Read the sentences in *italics* below the title of Chapter 1. Then look at the picture on page 3. What do you think?

a Where is Silas Marner?

....

b What is he thinking?

....

2 Read the new words at the bottom of page 2. Then answer these questions about the picture on page 3.

a What has the minister got in his hand?

....

b Is Silas behaving like a happy man or not?

....

c What is the minister thinking?

....

3 Read the new words at the bottom of page 3. Look at the picture on pages 4 and 5 and describe Silas's house and the land around it.

The Weaver of Raveloe

Dark thoughts drove all love out of his heart.
Because he was not a clever man, he stopped believing in a loving God.

As a young man, Silas Marner lived in a big town. He was a **weaver** and his friends were also weavers. They all went to the same church, in a place called Lantern Yard. At that time Silas Marner had a strong love of God and he went to church every Sunday. He was a good and honest man.

His best friend in Lantern Yard was William Dane. William was older than Silas and he, too, seemed a very fine young man. But William more often forgave his own **faults** than the faults of other people. He saw everyone's mistakes except his own. Even his teachers at school were sometimes wrong. But William Dane was always right.

Silas loved this young man and found no fault in him. He liked the fact that William was sure about everything. Silas was less sure of himself. He worried about his own faults. This difference between them showed in their faces. Silas's eyes shone with love but saw little; they were open and honest and almost too kind. William had a more secretive look in his narrow eyes.

weave /wiːv/ (v) to make cloth using a special machine. Pieces of cotton, for example, are passed over and under other pieces.
fault /fɔːlt/ (n) a problem or weakness in a person. If something bad is your *fault*, your actions are the reason for it.

One day Silas met a girl called Sarah. Soon he was in love with her and he wanted to marry her. She loved him and promised to become his wife. But they could not marry yet because they needed more money.

Sometimes Silas brought William with him when he met Sarah. There was no fear in his heart. He loved them both and he wanted them to be friends.

Then, one day, a bag of money was stolen from the church. Silas's knife was found in the church, so his house was searched. It was William who found the empty bag behind a cupboard in Silas's bedroom.

'It *was* you,' William said to his friend angrily. 'Tell the **truth** now!'

This hurt Silas deeply. 'William,' he said, 'I did not take the money. We are old friends. In nine years, I never once told you a lie. God will show us the truth.'

'Silas,' William replied, 'how could I know all your secrets? Sometimes a man seems honest, but deep in his heart he is bad.'

Silas looked at his friend, red in the face. Angry words were ready to pour from his mouth. But something stopped them. The red turned to white and his legs almost failed him. Finally, he spoke in a low voice.

'I remember now. The knife wasn't in my pocket.'

William said, 'I know nothing about that.'

The other people from the church wanted to know more, and asked a lot of questions. But Silas did not explain his words. 'I am in great trouble, but I can say nothing,' he told them. 'God will show you the truth.'

They returned to the church. They did not call in the police; that was not their way. 'But we have to find out the truth,' they all agreed. First they fell on their knees and asked God for help. Then one of them offered two white cards to Mr Paston, the **minister**. On top, the cards were the same. But one had a **mark** on the other side of it. The minister had to choose one of the cards.

'God will guide his hand. The minister will take the clean card,' said Silas to himself. 'But how can a man – a friend – **behave** so badly? I shall never forget that.'

Mr Paston chose one of the cards and held it up. It was the one with the mark. He spoke in a cold, hard voice. 'Silas Marner, you have done a terrible thing. You do not now belong to our church. You can only return to it if you give back the money. You will also have to say that you are sorry. And you will have to change your way of life.'

Silas listened without a word. He stood up only when the others started leaving their places. He went to William. He spoke with great difficulty.

truth /truːθ/ (n) the *true* facts about something
minister /ˈmɪnɪstə/ (n) someone who works for a Christan church
mark /mɑːk/ (n) a shape or sign on something; a hole or other sign that can be noticed
behave /bɪˈheɪv/ (v) to do things in the way that is described

'I remember that day when you wanted a knife. You used mine and you never gave it back to me. *You* took the money. You lied about me to protect yourself. But do not be afraid. God will not hurt *you*. He hurts only the good. He, too, is a God of lies.'

The church people never forgot these terrible words, but William replied calmly. 'You should not speak like that. But I shall only say "God forgive you", Silas.'

Silas left the church. It was the end of the world that he knew. Dark thoughts drove all love out of his heart. Because he was not a clever man, he stopped believing in a loving God.

'God has turned away from me,' he thought. 'Sarah will, too. If she does not, she will not be happy either. How can we be happy if God hates us?'

At home he sat alone. He was like a sick man; he could do nothing. He did not even want to see Sarah. 'She will never believe me. She won't be able to accept the truth, so she won't believe me,' he said to himself.

The next day he was working at his **loom** when the minister brought a message from Sarah. She did not want to marry Silas or to see him again. Silas said nothing. He turned back to his work.

Little more than a month later, Sarah married William Dane. Silas left the big town and moved to the village of Raveloe.

He lived there quietly for the next fifteen years. He lived and worked in a small house outside the village next to an old **quarry**. Nobody took stone from the quarry now, so it was full of water. Few of the villagers went near it. Silas was known as a very strange man, and they were a little afraid of him.

loom /lu:m/ (n) a machine used for making cloth
quarry /ˈkwɒri/ (n) a place where sand or stone is taken from the ground

CHAPTER 2

Love of Money

Slowly his interest in the gold and silver grew. Every new pound made him happy for a short time, but then he wanted more.

The village people knew nothing about Silas's secret. They were afraid of him for other reasons. He never invited them to his house, and he never drank with the other men in the village bar. The noise of the loom interested some of the village boys at first. They stood and listened outside Silas's house. When Silas saw them, he stepped down from his loom. He opened the door and, without a word, he fixed his large brown eyes on the boys. He looked hard at them because he could not see very well. But the boys did not know this. They ran away in fear. They knew from their mothers and fathers that Silas could help sick people. He had skills which were greater than those of other men. But when he was angry, there was danger in his eyes.

To add to his strange eyes, there was another mystery about Silas. Jem Rodney met him one evening at his gate and told his story later in the village bar.

'He was standing close to the gate. But he wasn't resting; there was a heavy bag on his back. His eyes were like a dead man's eyes. His arms and legs were as hard as stone. I spoke to him, and put my hand on him. He didn't move. "He's dead!" I said to myself. Then suddenly he was himself again. "Good night," he said, and walked away.'

The villagers talked about this, and they also, for a time, discussed his skills with the sick. One day Silas took an old pair of his shoes to the house of Mr Oates, the shoemender. Sally, Mr Oates's wife, was sitting by the fire. She looked very ill and Silas saw the signs of heart trouble. He felt sorry for her because he remembered the same terrible signs in his mother before her death. He remembered the name of the plant that slowed his mother's illness. He said to Sally, 'The doctor hasn't helped you. I believe that I can. I'll bring you something.'

After a few days, Sally Oates was much better. There was a lot of talk in the village. Soon all kinds of people were coming to Silas's house. There were mothers and their children and men from the farms. They all brought money. But Silas refused it. He was an honest man. Most of them wanted help which he could not give. He told them this, but they did not believe him. They continued to come. In the end he became angry and he drove them away.

And so Silas's kind act did not in the end bring him closer to the village people. They were angry with him too. After that, nobody went near his house and they left him alone.

But Silas was not interested in the village people. He was only interested in his work. He worked all day and far into the night. His troubles hurt him less when he worked hard. And because he was alone in the house, there was work of another kind. He cooked his own meals. He lit his own fire and carried water from the stream. In this way he drove out all thought from his life. He hated the past. He felt no love towards the people of Raveloe. He was without friends and without God.

Because he worked so hard, he earned a lot of money. He was the only weaver in Raveloe and he was paid for his work in gold and silver **coins**. He spent little on himself, but slowly his interest in the gold and silver grew. Every new pound made him happy for a short time, but then he wanted more. The coins were like friends and they seemed to know him. Every night he took them out and counted them. He loved their shape and colour and their shining faces.

Their home was in a metal pot under his loom. He took some stones out of the floor and made a hole. Each night, after counting the coins, he returned the pot to the hole. Then he put back the stones, and covered them with sand. This was not because he was afraid of thieves. Many country people saved their money and kept it in their houses. But nobody stole from their neighbours. They were not all honest, of course, but what could a thief do with the stolen money? He could only spend it in another part of England.

Year followed year, and Silas continued to live alone. He worked, and slowly filled the metal pot with coins. He watched them; and he worked. That was his life. No other thought, no other person had any part in it. The loom changed the shape of his back and of his arms and legs. When he left his work each evening, he could not stand up straight. He was not forty years old, but his face was dry and yellow like an old man's. The children called him "Old **Master** Marner".

But love was not quite dead in his heart. Every day he brought water from the stream. He carried it across two fields in a brown pot which he bought

coin /kɔːn/ (n) a piece of money made of metal
master /'mɑːstə/ (n) an old word for a skilled person who works with their hands

6

specially for this purpose. The pot always stood in the same place. He felt happy
when he touched it. When it was full, the water had a fresh, clear look. After
twelve years it was like a friend. And then, one day, he dropped it. It broke into
three pieces. With a heavy heart, Silas stuck the pieces together. The pot was no
use, but he put it in its old place. He wanted to remember it the way it was.

Fifteen years is a long time, but Master Marner's life showed little change.
He spent all day at work. At night he closed his doors and took out his money.
Because the metal pot could not hold it all, he moved the money into two
thick cloth bags. Out came the gold and silver pieces. How bright they were!
There was more gold than silver and he loved the gold pounds best. He spent
the small silver coins on his own needs. He pushed his hands through the piles
and counted every coin. He enjoyed feeling the shape of the coins between
his thumb and fingers. 'And others are on their way,' he said to himself, 'like
children who are not yet born. Year will follow year, and they will continue to
come.'

But soon a second great change came to Silas's life.

CHAPTER 3

The Sons of Squire Cass

She offered him everything: a good and happy life … But in a few weeks
of stupidity this possibility was lost to him.

The most important man in Raveloe was **Squire** Cass. He owned a lot of land with a number of farms on it. Farmers paid the Squire **rent** to live on the farms. So the Squire was quite rich. But his wife was dead and he preferred the village bar to his own house.

His sons got into bad company and soon learned bad ways. All rich young men enjoy themselves, but these two never did any work at all. The fault, the village said, was the Squire's; he did not teach them to behave.

Nobody liked the second son. His name was Dunstan but everybody called him "Dunsey". He was a rude young man who said terrible things about other people. He lied, and he drank like a fish.

Godfrey, the older son, was different. At first he was kind and honest. Everyone liked him. He wanted to marry Miss Nancy Lammeter, and the Raveloe people were pleased by this.

squire /skwaɪə/ (n) a man who, in the past, owned most of the land around a village
rent /rent/ (n) money that you pay someone for the use of their house or land

'He'll be a good squire when his father dies,' they said. 'And she'll be a good wife. They're a fine pair and she'll look after his money for him.'

Then Godfrey went away for a time. When he returned, he was a different person. His face no longer had its fresh colour and its honest look. Sometimes he was angry without reason. He was clearly hiding a secret.

'He's following the bad example of his brother,' people said. 'If he continues like this, Miss Lammeter won't marry him.'

One winter afternoon, Godfrey was alone in a dark room in his father's house. Clothes lay on chairs or on the floor. Dirty silver cups stood on the table and the fire was smoking. Godfrey was waiting for someone and there was an angry look on his face.

The door opened. A young man with a thick, heavy body came in. His face was red with drink and he was smiling for no reason. Godfrey gave him a look of hate. Godfrey's dog hurried away from the fire and hid in a corner.

'Well?' Dunsey asked. 'What do you want?'

'It's about Fowler,' Godfrey said angrily. 'You remember – he paid me his rent and I gave it to you. Now the Squire wants that money. If he doesn't get it this week, he'll go to the police. Then the true story will come out and you'll be in trouble.'

Dunsey's smile grew wider, but his eyes were hard. 'You'll be in trouble too,' he said. 'The Squire won't like your story about me, but he'll like my story about you even less. Don't forget – *you* married Molly Farren. *I* didn't. She's not exactly a nice young woman. And her life is an ugly one. And now you hate her. What will the Squire do if he hears that? You'll have to leave the house. All his money will come to me.' He smiled again and his voice changed. 'But if you're nice to me, I won't tell him,' he said. 'You'll have to pay Fowler's money to him. You'll get that hundred pounds, won't you?'

'How can I?' Godfrey cried. 'I haven't got any money. And you won't take my place here, either. If you talk, I'll talk too. Then we'll both have to leave.'

'No, we won't. You won't be so silly. You'll get the money and the Squire will have his rent.'

'I can't get the money!' Godfrey shouted.

'Sell your horse, Wildfire.'

'That'll take time. I need that money now.'

'Ride him to the **hunt** tomorrow. You'll get an offer for him there.'

'I don't want to come back late with dirt all over me. I'm going to Mrs Osgood's dance.'

'Aha!' Dunsey laughed. 'You want to see sweet Miss Nancy, do you?'

---

hunt /hʌnt/ (n/v) a careful search for someone or something. When you *hunt* wild animals, you want to kill them.

Godfrey's face was very red. 'Be quiet about Miss Nancy or I'll hit you!' he said angrily.

'Why?' asked Dunsey coldly. 'Let's talk about Nancy. Perhaps you'll be lucky. Molly may not live long. Then Nancy can be your second wife. That won't trouble her because she won't know. I won't tell her your secret. I won't tell her if you stay friendly with me.'

'Listen!' cried Godfrey angrily. 'I've had enough of this. If you continue, I shall tell the Squire everything. Then you can't trouble me again. Perhaps Molly will tell him that she's my wife. She said that once, when she was angry. Now she'll be even more angry. I can't give her money because you take it all. But I'm not going to paying your price this time. I'll tell my father everything. Keep the secret or don't keep it. It doesn't matter to me.'

Dunsey was afraid now, but he did not show it. 'Please yourself,' he said. He sat down and put his feet on another chair. Godfrey stood over him and his hands opened and closed. He was thinking hard. His body was large and strong and he was never afraid of a fight. But in matters of right and wrong he was less sure of himself.

He was very frightened. No plan could get him out of all his difficulties. After a little thought, he decided that he did not want to tell his father everything. He was angry with Dunsey, but he was more afraid of the Squire.

'What can I do, if my father drives me out?' he asked himself. 'I hate working. I'll lose Nancy. But I can't give up my drink and other amusements. Dunstan will always want money from me. But even that is better than life with no money or fun.'

Suddenly he spoke in an angry voice. '"Sell Wildfire", you say in your unfeeling way. I've never had a better horse. What will people think?'

Dunsey smiled. 'Send me to the hunt tomorrow. I'll sell Wildfire for you.'

'And run away with the money! No, thank you!'

'Please yourself,' said Dunsey quietly. 'It's not my business. You took the money from Fowler and lied to the Squire about it. I only wanted to help you.'

Godfrey walked angrily away. Then he came back. 'All right!' he cried. 'Sell Wildfire and bring me the money! If you don't, it's the end for you. In fact, we're both finished.'

Dunstan got up. 'You're being very sensible. I'll talk to Bryce. He'll pay a hundred and twenty pounds for the horse. You'll see.'

'And don't drink too much tomorrow, or you'll fall off. I'm not worried about you, but I *am* worried about Wildfire,' Godfrey told him.

'Don't worry. I never drink too much if I'm selling something. And I shan't hurt myself if I do fall.'

Dunstan closed the door noisily and left. Godfrey's thoughts returned to the reason for his problems. His sadness was greater because he was in love with Nancy Lammeter. She offered him everything: a good and happy life, a way of leaving his uncomfortable home and the people in it. But in a few weeks of stupidity this possibility was lost to him.

He did not love Molly, his wife. She was of low birth and could never take her place in his world. But she was pretty when he first met her. He married her because he was kind; he felt sorry for her. It was, of course, Dunstan who suggested it. Dunstan hated Godfrey and enjoyed using his brother's secret against him.

Godfrey's feelings of hate for his wife were growing. 'I can't have these thoughts,' he told himself. 'I'll go to the bar and listen to the talk. It doesn't interest me, but what can I do?'

His dog jumped up. She wanted him to put his hand on her head. But he pushed her away. Without a word or a look he left the room.

2.1 Were you right?

Look back at your answers to Activity 1.2 on page iv. Then finish these sentences.

Silas Marner, a hard-working and honest [1]....................................., is in love with Sarah. After money goes missing from the church, Silas's [2]................................ is found in the church and William Dane finds an empty bag in Silas's room. The people of the church want to find out the [3]................................ . When the minister chooses the card with the [4]................................ on it, he is angry. He wants Silas to give back the [5]................................ and to change his way of life. Then Silas remembers something important. [6]................................ used his knife and didn't give it back to him. When Silas leaves the church, he stops believing in [7]................................ . After Sarah marries the real thief, Silas moves to [8]................................ .

2.2 What more did you learn?

Finish these sentences. Draw a line from the names on the left to the words on the right.

1 Silas Marner

2 Squire Cass

3 Dunstan

4 Godfrey

5 Molly Farren

6 Nancy Lammeter

7 Wildfire

8 Bryce

a hates his brother, lies and drinks too much.

b is the woman who Godfrey loves.

c gave Fowler's rent money to his brother.

d is Godfrey's horse.

e loves money more than people or God.

f will pay £120 for Wildfire.

g is secretly married to Godfrey.

h is the most important man in Raveloe.

2.3 Language in use

**Look at the sentences in the box.
Then change these sentences using
past passive forms.**

> A bag of money **was stolen** from the church.
>
> Silas's knife **was found** in the church.

1 They searched his house.

His house ...was searched... .

2 They knew Silas as a very strange man.

Silas ....

3 They didn't call the police.

The police ....

4 The minister chose a card.

A card ....

5 Silas's medicine helped Sally.

Sally ....

6 Silas kept his money under the floor.

Silas's money ....

2.4 What happens next?

**Read the title of Chapter 4 and look at the pictures on pages 15 and 18. What
do you think will happen to this animal and these people?**

....

....

....

....

The Thief

'That's interesting! If he's dead, who will get his money? It's hidden, of course. Who knows the place?'

Next morning Dunstan Cass started early. On the way to the hunt, he rode past Silas Marner's house. The quarry was full of dirty red water. All around it, the earth was very wet. It was an ugly place. Dunstan could hear the noise of the loom. He remembered talk about Silas's money.

'Perhaps Marner can lend Godfrey some money,' he thought. 'Godfrey can pay him back later. He'll have a lot of money one day. Marner knows that. If he doesn't want to lend the money, I can change his mind. He'll be afraid of me. Godfrey can have his hundred pounds and more. Then he can give me some.'

But Dunstan did not stop. He wanted fun and the company of his friends.

When he reached the hunt, he met Bryce. 'Hello!' said Bryce. 'Why are you riding your brother's horse?'

Dunstan smiled and lied easily. 'Wildfire's my horse now,' he said. 'Godfrey gave me the horse because he owed me money. I didn't really want him, but it helped my brother. I had an offer for him a few days ago – a hundred and fifty pounds. But I shall keep him. He can jump everything – wall, gate or water.'

Bryce knew exactly what Dunstan was trying to do. 'You surprise me,' he said. 'Someone offers you more than its price and you refuse the offer. That's silly. You'll be lucky if you get a hundred.'

There was more talk. In the end Bryce offered a hundred and twenty pounds. 'You bring Wildfire to Batherley,' he said. 'Then you'll get the money.'

Dunstan accepted the offer, but he did not take the horse straight to Batherley. He had a drink with his friends first. Then he said to himself, 'I want to hunt. I don't want to wait in Batherley. There's no danger – I'm always lucky. Wildfire and I will show everyone some excitement.'

At first he enjoyed himself. He was in front, and he jumped the highest walls without trouble. Then he lost his way. Because he was angry, he took the next jump in a hurry. The horse fell and he fell with it. He was unhurt, but Wildfire died.

He thought only of himself and not of the horse. He did not want his friends to laugh at him. But nobody saw his fall. He had a drink from a bottle in his pocket and walked towards the nearest trees. Nobody could see him there and he could reach Batherley that way. At Batherley he could borrow a horse and ride home.

No thought of his brother or Wildfire troubled him. The idea of Marner's money interested him even more than before. He decided to walk home. He did not want to go to Batherley and answer questions about the horse. Evening was coming. In the dark a road was easier than a wood, and the road was quite close. He remembered seeing it a little before the accident. He remembered the signpost with "Raveloe" on it.

It was strange without a horse, but he was holding a riding stick. It really belonged to Godfrey and was borrowed without permission. He liked the feel of it and hit it once or twice against his boots.

He walked a long way and it grew dark. At last he saw a light. 'The quarry is probably not very far away,' he thought. 'Perhaps that's Marner's house. Shall I go and see him now? Godfrey won't ask him for money. He's too weak. But I'll get the money out of the old boy. Fear will do it if there's no other way. Perhaps he'll lend me a light too.'

In the dark and the rain the road was not very safe. So he turned towards the light. Slowly, he felt his way with his riding stick. He fell down two or three times, but at last he reached the door. He hit it loudly with his stick.

'That'll put fear in his heart,' he thought, laughing to himself. But no answer came; nobody moved inside the house. Was the weaver in bed? But the light was burning, and men like Marner did not use lights unnecessarily. Dunstan pushed the door hard. To his great surprise, it opened. There was a bright fire inside. He could see every corner of the room – the bed, the loom, the three chairs and the table. Marner was not there.

The fire looked welcoming. Dunsey went in and sat near it. A small piece of meat was cooking there. So the old man did not live on dry bread, but liked hot meat. It was hanging high up; he did not want it to cook too quickly. So he was out. But what was he doing outside on a wet night like this? Dunstan remembered his own difficulties on the road. His thoughts continued: 'Perhaps he only wanted to bring in wood for the fire. Perhaps he went too close to the quarry and fell in. That's interesting! If he's dead, who will get his money? It's hidden, of course. Who knows the place? And if someone takes the money, who will know?'

After these exciting questions came one that was even more exciting: 'Where *is* the money?' It drove all clear thought out of his head.

When country people hid their money, there were three favourite hiding places: the roof, the bed, and a hole in the floor. Marner's house had the wrong kind of roof. Quickly, Dunstan went towards the bed. On the way, his eyes searched the floor. Sand lay over the stones. It was not thick; he could see the shape of the stones without difficulty – except in one small place. Here the sand covered the stones completely. And the marks of fingers showed in the sand.

Dunstan hurried to the place. With his stick, he pushed away the sand and then tested the stones. They moved. Quickly, he lifted up two of them. There lay two cloth bags. 'They're very heavy!' he thought. 'They're probably full of coins.' He felt round the hole; but there were no more bags. Then he put the stones and the sand back.

All this took little more than five minutes, but to Dunstan it seemed a much longer time. Suddenly, he was afraid. He had to get out of the house into the dark. It was safer there. Dunstan picked up the bags and went out. He closed the door quickly behind him.

Outside, the night was darker and the rain was heavier than before.

He was pleased. But it was difficult to find his way. Both his hands were full. 'I mustn't fall,' he thought. 'But there's no need to hurry.' He stepped out into the dark.

CHAPTER 5

Silas's Pain

When he saw the empty hole, his heart gave a sudden jump.
It couldn't be true. But he felt a terrible fear.

When Dunstan Cass left the house, Silas Marner was not far away. An old piece of cloth kept the rain from his back. In his hand was a light. His legs were tired, but his heart held no thought of trouble or change.

Silas was thinking about the hot meal that was waiting for him. He liked meat, but he did not buy it himself. This was a present from Miss Priscilla Lammeter, and the Lammeters had only the best food. Other ladies also sometimes gave him presents when he brought their cloth to them.

The evening meal was his favourite. After it he looked at his gold. That night, his meal was almost ready when he remembered something. He needed more water for the next day. The weather was bad, and he did not want to leave his warm fire. But he could not spend time getting water in the morning. He did not want the meat to burn, so he pulled it higher up. Then he took his light and went out. He did not lock the door – he never thought of it.

When he returned, his eyes saw no change. He did not see the marks of Dunstan's feet, and soon his own footprints covered them. He moved the meat nearer to the fire. Then he sat down and warmed himself.

The fire lit up his pale face, his weak, tired eyes, and his thin body. He was so different from the people of Raveloe. That, perhaps, was the reason for their fear and dislike of him. Without the love of God or of friends, Silas had nothing – except his work and his money. The love of gold often drives a man to terrible actions. But poor Silas did not hurt anyone. The gold did not turn him into a bad man. It only kept him from the company of other men.

When he was feeling warm again, he could not wait any longer. He wanted to have the gold on the table during the meal. He got up and put a light on the floor near his loom. Then he pushed away the sand. He picked up the stones. When he saw the empty hole, his heart gave a sudden jump. It couldn't be true. But he felt a terrible fear. His hand started shaking. Quickly, he tried the hole again. Perhaps it was the fault of his eyes. Then he held the light in the hole. Every part of his body shook, and he dropped the light. He lifted his hands to his head and tried to think. Perhaps he moved his gold the night before, and then forgot? He did not, and he knew it. But he could not accept the truth; it was too terrible.

He searched in every corner. He turned his bed over and shook each sheet carefully. When he found nothing, he tried the hole again.

He stood up slowly. Perhaps it was a dream. He looked again at the table. He looked behind him and all round the room. He could see all the usual things in it – and the gold was not there.

Again he put his hands on his head, and he gave a loud cry. He walked with great difficulty to his loom, and sat in his usual seat.

'It's gone. A thief has taken my gold,' he said to himself. Then a new thought came to him. 'But one can catch a thief. If I catch this thief, I shall get my gold back.'

He went to the door and opened it. Very heavy rain was falling. Nobody could follow footprints in this weather.

'But when did the thief come?' Silas asked himself. 'When I went out this morning, I locked the door. I came back in the light and saw no footprints. And in the evening, too, there were no signs of a thief. Who in this village is a thief? Jem Rodney never seems very honest. And he takes birds from the Squire's fields and fish from his river. Everyone knows that. I often meet him near my house. He spoke to me about my money once. And another time he made an excuse and came into the house. He stayed a long time. Yes, he's the man. I will find him, and get my money back.'

This thought made Silas happier. He was not angry with Jem. He did not want to hurt him. But he wanted his gold back.

Silas knew little about matters of this kind. He thought about it for a few minutes. Finally, he said to himself: 'First, I should go and tell people the facts. Then the important people in the village – the **Rector**, the policeman and Squire Cass – will look for the thief. They will soon find out who he is. And if the thief doesn't give back the money, they will take it from him.'

When he had a clear plan, Silas ran out into the rain. He ran all the way to the village. Then, when he was too tired to run, he walked quickly. Soon he was at the village bar.

rector /ˈrektə/ (n) a church official in some Christian religions

CHAPTER 6

At the Village Bar

'Did you take my money?' Silas held up his hands. 'Give it to me!
Please! I'll – I'll give you a pound.'

T he villagers looked up from their glasses when Silas arrived at the door of
the bar. He did not speak, but looked at them with his strange eyes.

Some of the men were frightened. But Mr Snell, the barman, was not afraid.
'Master Marner!' he cried in a friendly way. 'What's the matter?'

Silas spoke with difficulty. 'A thief!' he said. 'My money! It's gone. I want a
policeman – and the Judge – and Squire Cass.'

Silas was very wet and seemed ill. 'Take hold of him, Jem,' the barman
ordered. 'He's not well. He'll fall.'

'Jem Rodney!' Silas turned his strange eyes on the man.

'What do you want?' Jem asked. He was afraid of Silas.

'Did you take my money?' Silas held up his hands. 'Give it to me! Please! I'll
– I'll give you a pound.'

'What?' Jem shouted angrily. He lifted his glass and prepared to throw it at Silas. 'Say that again and you'll be sorry!'

'Let's not have talk like that, Master Marner.' Mr Snell took Silas's arm. 'Calm down and we shall listen to the facts. Now – sit down here.' He took off Silas's wet coat and pushed him into a chair near the fire. 'Now, Master Marner.' He sat down at Silas's side. 'What's all this about a thief?'

Slowly, Silas told his story and answered all their questions. His problem was clear to all of them and they began to change their minds about him. He was only a simple man like them.

When he finished, Mr Snell put a hand on his arm. 'It's a terrible thing,' he said. 'And we're all sorry for you. But you mustn't talk like that to Jem Rodney, Master Marner. Perhaps he does eat another man's fish from time to time. But he's been here all evening like an honest man.'

Silas suddenly remembered his own trouble long ago, and he was sorry. He got up and went to Jem. 'I was wrong,' he said. 'I spoke without thinking. But you were in my house more often than the others. I'm sorry.' His voice sounded tired and sad.

'That's all right, Master Marner,' Jem said.

'How much money was in the bags?' another man asked. His name was Mr Dowlas.

'More than two hundred and seventy-two pounds. I counted it last night.' Silas sat down again in his chair.

'That's not very heavy,' a man said. 'Someone was passing through Raveloe and he took the money. A homeless person, perhaps, who moves from place to place.'

'Why were there no footprints? Why did the stones and sand show no sign of anyone?' Mr Dowlas continued. 'I'll tell you. You can't see very well, Master Marner. Now, I have a plan. You and I and another man will get the policeman. We'll all go to your house and search it. Then, perhaps, we'll find some signs of the thief.'

The barman went to the door and opened it. 'The rain's heavy,' he said.

'I'm not afraid of the rain,' said Mr Dowlas. 'And Judge Malam will be very unhappy if we don't do anything.'

'You're right,' agreed the barman. 'Someone has to go.'

'I'll go with you.' Jem Rodney stood up.

'Good,' said Mr Dowlas. 'Are you ready, Master Marner?'

The barman helped Silas to his feet and gave him an old coat. Silas looked around the room. There was no hope in his brown eyes. The two men were waiting by the door. He put on his coat and followed them into the rain.

3.1 Were you right?

Look back at Activity 2.4. Then finish these sentences.

1 After Dunstan jumps too quickly, Wildfire dies .

2 Dunstan finds Silas's hiding-place because ....
....

3 Because both Dunstan's hands are full, ...
....

4 Silas is not in the house because ....
....

5 When Silas sees the empty hole, ...
....

6 Jem Rodney's name comes to Silas's mind because ....
....

3.2 What more did you learn?

1 **Who says the words below in the village bar? Put the letters of the sentences under the correct pictures.**

a 'Give it to me! Please! I'll – I'll give you a pound.'

b 'Say that again and you'll be sorry.'

c 'What's all this about a thief?'

d 'I was wrong. I spoke without thinking.'

e 'The rain's heavy.'

f 'I'll go with you.

2 **Discuss the sentences above with another student. Why does the speaker say them?**

3.3 Language in use

Read the sentences in the box. Then make one sentence from the pairs below, using the word *if*.

> 'You**'ll be** lucky **if** you **get** a hundred.'
>
> Fear **will do** it **if** there**'s** no other way.

1 He will be dead. Who will get the money?

   If ..*he is dead, who will get the money?*..

2 Someone will take the money. Who will know?

   If ....

3 I will get my gold back. I will catch this thief.

   If ....

4 Judge Malam will be very unhappy. We will do nothing.

   If ....

5 Silas won't be able to count his coins each night. How will he feel?

   If ....

3.4 What happens next?

Read the titles of Chapters 7, 8 and 9 and the sentences in *italics* under each. What do you think? Circle *Yes* or *No*.

1 Bryce will tell Godfrey about Wildfire.   Yes   No

2 Dunstan will return home and fight with Godfrey.   Yes   No

3 Godfrey will tell his father about Fowler's money.   Yes   No

4 The Squire will be angry with Godfrey and Dunstan.   Yes   No

5 Silas's neighbour will visit him because she wants to marry him. Yes   No

6 Silas will start going to church again.   Yes   No

7 Silas's money will be found.   Yes   No

8 Godfrey will tell his father about his wife, Molly.   Yes   No

CHAPTER 7

The Hunt for the Thief

'Nothing hurts him!' Godfrey said angrily. 'He hurts others.'
He looked away from Bryce and his face was troubled.

N ext morning, everyone was talking about the thief. Godfrey listened to the talk and visited the quarry. The ground was wet and showed no clear footprints. But a small **tinder-box** was lying near the house. Inside it, there were pieces of stone and metal for making a fire.

It was not Silas's tinder-box. His was standing in its place in his house. 'It was the thief's. He dropped it,' most people said. But others did not agree. They could not accept Silas's strange story. 'You'll see,' they said. 'Silas took the money himself. Perhaps he didn't have any. He's half crazy, isn't he?'

At the bar, Squire Cass and the Rector, Mr Crackenthorp, were talking to Mr Snell. Mr Snell was telling the other two about the box.

'When I first heard about the tinder-box,' he said, 'I didn't remember this. About a month ago, a **pedlar** visited Raveloe. The pedlar was thirsty and he came to the bar. He carried a tinder-box like that one. He used it when he smoked. Was the box near Marner's house the pedlar's tinder-box, do you think?'

When they heard about this, the village people took the greatest interest in the pedlar. But Silas could remember nothing about him. 'Yes,' he said to the Squire and the Rector. 'The pedlar came to my door. But he didn't come into the house. I didn't want anything and so he left.' Silas wanted the pedlar to be the thief. He wanted them to search for him. But he could not lie about the man because he was too honest.

People were sorry about Silas's reply. Some were even a little angry. 'Of course it was the pedlar,' they said. 'He didn't go away. He hid and waited. While he was waiting, he dropped the tinder-box by accident. Marner didn't see him because Marner can't see anything. These pedlars are very quick. He only needed one look at Marner's face to see that half-crazy look in it. It's the look of someone who loves money. Marner's lucky that he wasn't killed. Men like the pedlar often kill for money.'

Godfrey Cass did not agree. He heard the talk about the pedlar in the bar. 'I don't think that it was the pedlar,' he said. 'I bought a knife from the man. He had quite a nice smile. He wasn't a bad man at all.'

---

tinder-box /'tɪndə bɒks/ (n) a box for holding small pieces of wood and other dry things. These are used to start a fire.
pedlar /'pedlə/ (n) someone who, in the past, sold small things at people's doors. *Pedlars* walked from place to place.

But Godfrey was not interested in the thief. Dunstan was not at home and his fears were growing. 'Has he had an accident?' Godfrey thought to himself. 'Perhaps he's sold the horse, and is spending the money. He'll come back in a month without anything. I know him so well. Why did I give him Wildfire?'

He borrowed a horse and rode towards Batherley. There, perhaps, he could hear some news of Dunstan. Suddenly, he saw another man on a horse and his heart gave a jump. Was it Dunstan on Wildfire? He rode more quickly.

But it was Bryce. Godfrey did not like the look on his face. Bryce rode to Godfrey and stopped.

'Your brother's a lucky man, isn't he?' Bryce asked.

'Lucky? Why?'

'Hasn't he come home?'

'No.' Godfrey's fears were growing. 'What's he done with the horse?'

'I offered him a hundred and twenty pounds for it.' Bryce sounded troubled. 'It was a very high price, but I've always liked Wildfire. And what did he do? He rode it at a very high wall. The horse fell and it was killed. And Dunsey hasn't come home?'

'No.' Godfrey was very angry. 'So he's killed my horse. If he has any sense, he'll stay away.'

'Ah!' Bryce said. 'I wasn't sure. I thought that Dunsey was selling it without permission.'

'He did have my permission,' Godfrey told him.

'Then where is he?' Bryce said. 'Nobody has seen him in Batherley. And the fall didn't hurt him, because he walked away.'

'Nothing hurts *him!*' Godfrey said angrily. 'He hurts others.' He looked away from Bryce and his face was troubled. 'I was going to Batherley,' he said. 'But there's no need now. You've told me enough. Are you coming to Raveloe?'

'No, not now,' Bryce answered. 'I've told you about the horse.' He thought for a minute. 'Perhaps Dunsey's afraid of you and is visiting the bar in Whitbridge. He likes the place.'

'Perhaps,' said Godfrey. His heart was heavy. 'He'll be back.'

'I'll leave you now,' Bryce said. 'I'm very sorry about Wildfire. Goodbye.' He rode away.

Godfrey rode home slowly. Next morning he should tell his father about Dunsey and the money. 'I'll tell him everything,' he thought. 'I'll tell the truth. I'll have to tell him about my wife. I know that Dunsey will come back. If I don't tell the Squire about Molly, Dunsey will. The Squire's a hard man and he'll send me away. I'll lose Nancy and everyone will know about my past.'

He went to sleep late that night. 'At last I've decided,' he thought. 'It won't be easy, but it's the right thing to do.'

But in the morning his old fears came back. 'I can't do it,' he thought. 'Everyone will talk about me. And I *can't* lose Nancy. Nothing was clear to me yesterday, because I was so angry with Dunstan. I need to stay friendly with him. I need his help, so I'll make excuses for him. Then my father won't be too angry. That's the best plan. If I'm lucky, Dunstan will stay away. Then my secret will be safe. This way, everything will be all right.'

CHAPTER 8

Father and Son

The Squire's face was red and angry, and he spoke with difficulty.
'You gave Dunsey the money? Why? Are you both thieves?'

Godfrey had an early breakfast and waited for his father. At last the Squire arrived. He was sixty years old and a big, tall man. He was different from the other Raveloe farmers. He was very sure of himself: his voice and his straight back showed this. Because he met nobody from a better family than his, he behaved like the most important man in the country.

'What are you waiting for?' he asked his son. Few polite words were spoken in the Casses' house.

'I wanted to speak to you, sir,' Godfrey said.

'What about?' The Squire started to eat his breakfast.

'It's about Wildfire,' Godfrey told him.

'You've had a fall, have you? Now you want some money for a horse doctor. *My* father wasn't always paying out money to his sons. Too much money is going out and not enough is coming in. People are late with their rents. Fowler promised me a hundred pounds last month, but I haven't got it. If he gives me any trouble about the rent, I'll throw him out!'

Godfrey felt even more frightened. But he continued: 'Wildfire isn't hurt, sir; he's dead. Dunsey took him to the hunt a few days ago. I wanted him to sell the horse for me. Bryce offered him a hundred and twenty pounds for Wildfire. But the horse was killed, so I can't pay you the hundred pounds.'

'Pay me?' The Squire was surprised and angry. 'Why? What hundred pounds are you talking about?'

'Fowler *did* pay his rent, sir,' Godfrey explained. 'He paid me last month when I was at his house. But Dunsey wanted the money and I gave it to him. I wanted to pay you back before this.'

The Squire's face was red and angry, and he spoke with difficulty. 'You gave Dunsey the money? Why? Are you both thieves? Explain yourself. Where is Dunsey? Go and bring him.'

'He hasn't come back, sir.'

'Why not? Did he hurt himself?'

'No, sir. He walked away from the accident. But nobody knows where he is now.'

'If *he* can't explain, *you* will!' The angry Squire hit the table. 'Why did you give him the money?'

'I – I don't know, sir.'

'You don't know? Of course you know!' The Squire had a sudden idea. 'I know. You did something terrible and you don't want him to tell me.'

Godfrey was really frightened when he heard this. It was the truth. But he hid his fear and spoke lightly. 'It was only a little thing. A young man's amusement is not important.'

'Don't talk to me about a young man's amusement,' the Squire said angrily. 'You're not so young now and I won't accept any more of this. Your way of life has to change. I can't continue paying for your fun and games. Why can't I enjoy a more comfortable life? Because we never have enough money. How can we have enough money? You don't help me with the work here.'

'I often offer my help, sir,' Godfrey said quietly. 'But you get angry with me. "It's *my* place and *I'll* give the orders", you tell me.'

'I don't remember that,' the Squire said. 'But I do remember one thing. Some time ago, you wanted to marry Lammeter's daughter. I didn't put difficulties in your way like many fathers. The girl is as good as another. So what's the problem? She hasn't refused you, has she?'

'No,' said Godfrey, feeling very uncomfortable. 'But I think she will.'

'You *think*? Why don't you ask her? You want her, don't you?'

Godfrey looked away. 'Yes,' he said quietly. 'Very much.'

'If *you're* not man enough, *I'll* ask Lammeter. He won't refuse *my* family.'

'Please don't do that, sir!' cried Godfrey in great fear. 'Nancy's angry with me now. And *I* want to speak to her. It's a man's **duty.**'

'Well – do it soon! And live a better life. A wife always asks for that.'

'There are other difficulties too, sir.' Godfrey thought hard before he spoke. 'You don't want to give me one of the farms, do you? Nancy won't want to live in this house with all of us.'

'Won't she?' said the Squire with a hard laugh. 'Ask her. You'll soon see.'

'I need to wait, sir. Please don't say anything to Mr Lammeter in a hurry.'

'If I want to, I shall,' said the Squire. 'I give the orders here. Now I'm going out. Oh! There's another thing. Sell Dunsey's horse and give me the money, will you? He'll keep no more horses at my cost. And when you see him, give him a message. He needn't come back here. He can find work and pay for himself. Now, go and order my horse.'

Godfrey left the room. 'That's the end of that,' he thought. 'Am I pleased or sorry? I don't know. Perhaps I've only brought new trouble on myself. If Father speaks to Mr Lammeter about Nancy, I can't refuse her. What can I do then? I can't marry her. I can't do anything – except wait. Yes, that's it. I'll wait. Perhaps something will change and then everything will get better.'

duty /'djuːti/ (n) something that you have to do

CHAPTER 9

Good Neighbours

*'It's never too late, Master Marner. Come to church and perhaps
the result will surprise you.'*

Judge Malam was an important man. 'He's cleverer than any of us,' people in Raveloe always said. The Judge thought so too. He listened to the reports about the thief, and the tinder-box interested him greatly. He gave his orders and soon a description of the pedlar was sent to all the villages in the area. But nobody knew the pedlar's name and he was never found.

There was talk in the village too, when Dunstan Cass did not come back. This was not the first time. Once, after angry words with his father, he left and did not return for six weeks. Dunstan Cass and Silas's gold went missing on the same day. But nobody put these two facts together. Christmas was near; the holiday was in everyone's thoughts. And who could speak against the Casses – the oldest and most important family in Raveloe?

But Christmas brought no end to the pain in Silas's heart. He could only think about one thing. His gold was his only interest in life. Without it, he was the saddest of men. His life was empty. The loom was there, of course, and he continued to make cloth. But where was his money? It was not under his feet in the daytime or in his hands at night. Even the thought of his next earnings did not make him feel better. 'What's the use of it?' he thought. 'It will be so little, and I had so much. I'll never have so much again.'

In the evenings, he sat alone by his small fire. His head rested on his knees. He cried quietly. He did not want anyone to hear him.

But the village did not forget him. The Rector and the richer families sent him presents of Christmas food. Poorer people greeted Silas in the village. They talked about his trouble and they visited his house. When Silas told them his story, they said, 'Well, your money has gone, but there are other poor people around here. And when you can't work, you'll get help. There's money for people who need it.' But they did not make Silas feel better.

One evening, Mr Macey visited Silas. He, too, wanted to help. He sat down in his slow, important way and talked for a time. Then he said, 'Will you listen to me for a minute, Master Marner?'

Silas looked at him with his sad, brown eyes. 'I'll try,' he said.

'Have you got a Sunday suit?'

'No.'

'Buy one. Tookey will make you a suit at a low price. You can pay for it later. Then you can come to church like other people. You should come soon, or it will be too late. That's what I think.' Mr Macey talked to Silas for a little longer and then he left.

Mrs Winthrop also visited Silas. She was a woman with an honest heart who always did her duty. She finished her housework very early. Then she looked for ways of helping others. Women of this kind are sometimes difficult and unwelcome, but Dolly Winthrop was a kind person. Families always asked for her help in times of trouble. They welcomed her warm heart. She was a pretty woman, but there was something quiet and sad about her.

After his trouble, Silas was often in this good woman's thoughts. One Sunday afternoon she went to see him with her little boy, Aaron. She took some cakes with her. Everyone in Raveloe liked the taste of her cakes.

Silas opened his door without saying a word. Then he moved a chair and made a sign. Dolly sat down. She showed Silas the cakes and said with a smile, 'I made them yesterday, Master Marner. The cakes are very good. Perhaps you'll enjoy some.' She held out the cakes to Silas and he thanked her. Then, in his usual way, he put them close to his weak eyes to look at them. Aaron watched in surprise. He was hiding behind his mother's chair.

'Didn't you hear people going to church this morning, Master Marner?' Dolly asked. 'Perhaps your loom makes too much noise.'

'Yes, I heard them,' Silas replied.

'Well, you poor man,' said Dolly, 'why work on Sunday? Of course, you need to cook a hot meal. Everyone has a hot meal on Sundays. But the shop will cook your meat and it only costs two pence. Why don't you come to church on Christmas Day? The church will look beautiful and there'll be music and songs.'

'I don't know anything about the church,' Silas replied.

'Don't you?' Dolly asked. She was a little surprised. She waited for a minute and then continued, 'Well, it's never too late, Master Marner. Come to church and perhaps the result will surprise you. I always feel so happy in church. And if trouble comes, it won't hurt me. That's because I ask for God's help. We all have to do that. If we do our duty, He won't fail us.'

Silas did not agree with Dolly at all but he said nothing. He did not want to go to church. And he never spoke much except about business matters.

By this time, Aaron was less afraid of the weaver. He moved towards him a little. Silas saw him at his mother's side. He offered him a piece of cake. Aaron moved back quickly – then held out his hand.

'What are you thinking, Aaron?' said his mother, but she took him on her knees. 'You don't want cake *again*, do you? He loves his food,' she continued. 'He's my youngest child, and we can't refuse him anything. His father and I always want him near us.'

She put her hand on Aaron's brown head. 'His pretty face will make Master Marner happier,' she thought. But Silas could only see his face with great difficulty.

'And he's got a beautiful voice,' Dolly went on. 'His father's taught him a Christmas song. He learnt very quickly. And that's a good sign, because it's a good song. Now, Aaron, stand up and sing the song to Master Marner.'

Aaron made no reply, but put his head on his mother's arm.

'Oh, that's rude,' said Dolly. 'Mother said "Stand up." I'll hold your cake.'

Because his mother was near, Aaron was not too frightened. Also, he wanted to sing to Silas. He was a little afraid of strange Master Marner, and he looked at him hard. Then he stood behind the table, so only his head showed. When he began the song, his voice was as clear as a bird's.

Dolly listened happily, and looked at Silas. 'He'll want to come to church, now,' she thought.

When Aaron finished, she gave him the cake. 'No other music is as good as Christmas music,' she said. 'And ask yourself this question, Master Marner: "How will it sound in church?" There'll be many more voices in church. It's beautiful. The boy has a pretty voice, hasn't he?'

'Very pretty,' Silas agreed. He was not really interested. But he wanted to show some sign of thanks, so he offered Aaron more cake.

'No, thank you,' Dolly said. 'We should go now and I'll say goodbye. But if you're ever ill, I'll come. I'll clean the house and get your food. I'll be pleased to do it. But please don't weave on a Sunday. You'll only have bad thoughts and a sick body.'

Silas thanked Dolly for her kind help. But he was pleased when she left. He could go back to his work.

And he did not listen to her or to Mr Macey. He stayed at home on Christmas Day. He ate his meat with a sad heart. Outside, there was ice and a strong wind. In the evening, snow fell and the darkness closed round him.

But the other villagers went to church that day. After church, they walked home. They walked quickly, because it was so cold. The rest of the day was free. They could eat, drink and enjoy themselves.

At Squire Cass's family party, nobody spoke Dunstan's name. Nobody was sorry that he was not there. Most of the talk was the same every year. Uncle Kimble, the doctor, told exciting stories about his early life in London. Games of cards followed the stories. Aunt Kimble made her usual mistakes. Uncle Kimble became angry when he lost.

But the party on Christmas Day was only a small, quiet one. The real party of the season was on the day before the New Year. In the evening, the Casses always held a great dance. It was a time to end all disagreements from the past year. They invited all their old friends from far and near.

Godfrey Cass thought about this dance with both hope and fear. 'Next year, Dunsey may come back and tell my father about my wife,' he thought. 'Perhaps my father will learn the secret in another way. But at the dance I'll see Nancy again. I can talk to her and dance with her.' There was some hope in that thought.

4.1 Were you right?

Look back at your answers to Activity 3.4. What do you know about Godfrey, Dunstan and Silas now? Talk to other students and write notes about these people.

Notes

4.2 What more did you learn?

Read these sentences and write the missing words.

Near Silas's house, a ¹ .... is found. Mr Snell remembers that about a month ago a ² .... visited Raveloe. He used a similar one when he smoked. Silas wants this stranger to be the ³ ...., but the man is never found.

Godfrey learns that ⁴ .... is dead. The Squire wants Godfrey to ⁵ .... Nancy Lammeter. If his son will not ask Nancy, the Squire will ask her ⁶ .... But Godfrey says it is his ⁷ .... to speak to Nancy. The Squire does not want ⁸ .... to live in his house again.

Mr Macey and Mrs Winthrop ask Silas to go to ⁹ .... But Silas stays at home alone on ¹⁰ .... Day.

4.3 Language in use

Look at the sentences in the box.
Make sentences using past progressive
forms of the verbs.

> Next morning everyone **was talking** about the thief.
>
> At the bar, Squire Cass and the Rector ... **were talking** to Mr Snell.

enjoy	go	grow
lie	tell	wait

1 A small tinder-box ......was lying...... near the house.

2 At the bar, Mr Snell .... the other men about the box.

3 While the pedlar ...., he dropped the tinder-box by accident.

4 Dunstan was not at home and Godfrey's fears ....

5 'I .... to Batherley but there's no need now.'

6 The people .... the church while Silas sat at home.

4.4 What happens next?

Look at the pictures on pages 36, 39 and 41. What do you think is happening?
Discuss them with another student. Then write one or two sentences about
each picture.

1 (page 36) ....

....

....

....

2 (page 39) ....

....

....

....

3 (page 41) ....

....

....

....

CHAPTER 10

A New Year in Raveloe

She needed help, but she had no friend except opium. She wanted to
feed the child in her arms, but she was tired and ill.

Everyone enjoyed the party. There were a lot of good things to eat. Old friends met again; people made new friends. There was dancing, music, drink and happy talk. And Godfrey's dreams came true. He found himself alone with Nancy.

He danced with her until the Squire accidentally stepped on her long dress. Priscilla, Nancy's sister, promised to repair the dress. So Godfrey took Nancy to a small room away from the dancing and they waited there for Priscilla.

'You needn't stay,' Nancy told Godfrey coldly. 'I'll be all right.'

'But I want to stay,' Godfrey said.

'You'll miss the next dance,' Nancy said.

'That doesn't matter. I want to be with you. That's more important.'

'You surprise me!'

'Can't you forgive me, Nancy?' Godfrey took a step towards her. 'I often behave badly, but I want to change.'

'Change is a good thing.' Nancy's voice was a little softer. 'But it's always better if no change is necessary.'

'You've got a hard heart, Nancy. I want to be better, but you don't help me. I'm unhappy and it doesn't matter to you.'

'How can you talk about hard hearts? Who behaved badly first? How much do I really matter to you?'

Nancy's angry words pleased Godfrey. Perhaps she loved him, even now. But then Priscilla hurried in. 'Do I have to go?' he asked.

'Please yourself,' said Nancy. She looked down at her dress.

'I'll stay,' said Godfrey. 'Tomorrow is not important,' he thought. 'I'll enjoy tonight.'

In Nancy's company, Godfrey Cass forgot his wife. But Godfrey was the only person in his wife's mind. She was walking slowly through the snow on the Raveloe road. Her child was in her arms.

She was remembering an angry speech of Godfrey's: 'I will never take you to Raveloe. I don't want my family or my friends to meet you. I will die first.' Molly never forgave him for those words. She knew about the great New Year party, and she had a plan.

'So he'll leave me here, will he?' she said to herself. 'He'll hide me away, and enjoy himself with his fine friends. But I'll put an end to his enjoyment. I'll show the Squire his oldest son's wife. They can all see my dirty clothes. They can all see my tired face – and I was pretty. They can all see my little child. They will see that it has its father's hair and eyes.'

Godfrey sent money to Molly, and she had enough for good clothes. She knew this. But she spent all her money on **opium**, and she hated her husband. When she took the opium, she forgot her troubles. She forgot everything except her child. Opium is a terrible thing. At first you enjoy it, but soon you cannot live without it. In the end, it destroys you. It was destroying Molly. She loved her child. But she did not always remember to feed it.

It was seven o'clock and she was not very far from Raveloe. But she did not know this. There was no sign of an end to the road. She needed help, but she had no friend except opium. She wanted to feed the child in her arms, but she was tired and ill. She took a piece of opium from her pocket and ate it.

She walked with more and more difficulty. The wind was like ice, but now she did not feel it. She forgot her plan, her duty to her child, everything. She just wanted to sleep. She left the road, and lay down under a small tree. The snow was soft. Her arms were holding the child and it did not wake.

But when deep sleep came, the mother's arms and fingers opened. The little head fell back and the blue eyes looked up. The child gave a little cry; it missed its mother's arms. But she heard nothing. Suddenly, the child forgot her

opium /ˈəʊpiəm/ (n) a very strong drug made from plants

mother, forgot the cold snow. A light was moving across the white ground. It came towards the child, but never reached her. She felt that she had to catch the beautiful light. On hands and knees, she moved towards it. She couldn't catch it in the snow. She lifted her head; the light was coming from a place not far away. The little one got up and walked through the snow. An old, dirty piece of cloth covered her dress. Part of it hung down behind her and moved across the ground.

The little one continued walking until she came to Silas's open door.

The light came from his fire. She sat down in front of it and warmed her hands. She did not miss her mother because she often played alone. At first she made happy little noises to the fire. But soon all of her was warm. The little golden head touched the floor and the blue eyes closed.

But where was Silas? Earlier in the day, someone told him to listen to the singing from the church. 'If you listen at New Year, perhaps it will bring you luck. Perhaps your money will come back.' So Silas was outside, listening to the songs.

While he was outside, he suddenly felt ill and weak. For some time he saw nothing and heard nothing. When the feeling left him, he went back inside. He closed the door, returned to the fire and sat down. Suddenly, in the fire's weak light, he saw something gold on the floor. Was it – surely not – his own gold? He felt so excited that he could not move.

At last he put out his hand. But his fingers did not feel the usual hard shape of coins. They touched soft, warm hair. Silas fell on his knees in surprise. He put his head down, and saw the child asleep. All over its head was hair that was the colour of gold.

'Is this my little sister?' was Silas's first thought. 'Has she come back in a dream? I carried her in my arms when she was small. But she died when I was a boy. *Is* this a dream?'

He pushed the sticks in the fire together, and threw on new ones. Soon the fire was giving more light. The child was there on the floor. The little round shape and the old clothes were clear to his eyes. She looked very similar to his sister.

'How did she get in, and why didn't I see her?' he thought to himself. He could not answer the questions, and thought made him tired. He sat back in his chair, and closed his eyes. He remembered his sister and his old home, the old streets and Lantern Yard.

Suddenly, there was a cry. The child was awake and wanted her mother. Silas lifted her onto his knees. She hung round his neck and gave louder cries. Silas held her tightly and made calming sounds.

He was very busy in the next hour. He warmed some of his own food. He found some brown sugar and added that. Then he fed the child with a spoon.

Her cries stopped and her blue eyes opened wide. After a time, she got off his knee. She took a few steps, but she could not stand up very well. Silas jumped up, and followed her. He did not want her to fall and hurt herself. But she only sat back on the floor and pulled at her shoes. Her little face had an angry look. Silas took her on his knee again. He knew nothing about the troubles of small children. But at last he understood. The tight, wet shoes were hurting her warm feet. With difficulty, he took the shoes off. The little girl looked at her toes and laughed. They were a joke and a mystery. She showed them to Silas.

He was holding the wet shoes. 'She came in from the snow,' he suddenly thought. He lifted up the child. He carried her to the door and opened it. Then she remembered her mother again, and cried out for her. He put his head down to look at the ground. With difficulty, he saw her little footprints in the snow. He followed them into the trees. She held out her hands, and tried to jump out of his arms. She was crying again and again for her mother. At last he saw a shape. He knew without a second look that it was a body. The head was under a tree, resting on the ground. It was almost covered in snow.

CHAPTER 11

The End of a Marriage

Her wide blue eyes looked up at Godfrey, but gave no sign.
He was half pleased and half sorry when she did not know him.

A t the Squire's house, the guests were talking and dancing happily. The Squire was at the centre of a group of friends. He was laughing and telling them a joke. Godfrey stood against the wall. He was watching Nancy and hoping for another dance with her. For a second, he turned his eyes away and looked towards the door.

A sudden cold fear came into his heart. He saw Silas and he saw his own child in Marner's arms. 'No!' he said softly. But there was no mistake. The child with the golden hair was his.

Other people's eyes began to fall on Silas. The Rector and Mr Lammeter hurried across to him. Godfrey followed them slowly. His face was white.

'Marner!' the Squire called. 'What are you doing here? What do you want?' The room grew quiet.

'I need the doctor,' Silas said.

'What's wrong?' asked the Rector.

'It's a woman,' Silas told him. 'She's in the snow near my door. She's dead – or almost dead.'

'Don't talk about it here,' said the Rector. 'Think of the ladies. We don't want to worry them. Go into that room there. I'll bring Doctor Kimble to you.'

But by this time there was a crowd of ladies around Silas. They showed great interest in the pretty child. She was half afraid of so many people and all the lights. But they excited her too. Sometimes she smiled and sometimes she hid her face.

'Whose child is it?' Nancy asked Godfrey. She was standing next to him now. He turned and looked at her. He could not speak immediately. Then he said, 'I don't know. He found a woman in the snow. He says that the child is hers.'

'Why don't you leave the poor child here, Master Marner?' suggested kind Mrs Kimble. She looked at the child's dirty clothes. 'Someone will look after her.'

'No – no – I can't leave her!' Silas held the child more tightly. 'She's come to me and I'll look after her.'

Doctor Kimble came in from the card room. He spoke to the Squire and then hurried out. Godfrey followed him. 'Get me a pair of thick shoes, Godfrey, will you?' Doctor Kimble asked. 'And someone should run and find Dolly Winthrop. She's the best person for this kind of problem.' He hurried away with Silas.

'I'll go,' Godfrey said quickly. 'I'll bring Mrs Winthrop.' Godfrey hurried away too. He took his hat and coat. But he forgot that he was wearing his dancing shoes.

A few minutes later, he and Dolly were walking quickly towards the quarry. 'You go back, sir,' she said. 'You'll get wet feet and then you'll be ill.'

'No, I'll wait here,' said Godfrey. They were outside Marner's house. 'Tell me if I can do anything.'

'Yes, sir,' said Dolly, and went into the house.

Godfrey did not really hear her. He did not think about his wet feet or the icy cold. He had only one thought. 'Is Molly dead?' he asked himself again and again. 'Can I marry Nancy now? Then I don't need to have any more secrets. There's the child, of course. I'll look after her. I'll find a way. But perhaps Molly will live. If she does, I'll have no possibility of a happy life.'

Godfrey waited, without any idea of the time. At last Uncle Kimble came out. Godfrey hid his thoughts and walked towards him.

'I was here, so I waited,' he said.

'There was no need. Why didn't you send one of the men? I can't do anything: she's dead.'

Godfrey's heart raced. 'What kind of woman is she?' he asked.

'She's a young woman, but very thin. Her hair is long and black. She had no money, and she needed new clothes. But she was wearing a wedding ring. They'll take her away tomorrow. I'm going back now. Come with me.'

'I want to look at her,' said Godfrey. 'I saw a woman like that yesterday. I'll join you later.'

He went into the room where his wife lay. He hated her while she lived. But now she was dead. He took only one look at her. Sixteen years later, when he told the full story of this night, he remembered every line on her sad, tired face.

He turned to the fire. Silas was sitting there with the child in his arms. She was quiet, but not asleep. Her wide blue eyes looked up at Godfrey, but gave no sign. He was half pleased and half sorry when she did not know him. The blue eyes turned away from him slowly. They looked back at the weaver's strange face. A small hand gave a soft pull at Silas's ear.

'You'll take the child to the children's home tomorrow?' Godfrey's voice did not show his interest.

'Who says that?' said Silas quickly. 'Do I have to take her?'

'You don't want to keep her, do you? You're old and unmarried.'

'Nobody will take her away from me, except her family. And there's no sign of a family. The mother's dead, and the child clearly has no father. She's alone – and I'm alone.'

'Poor little child!' said Godfrey. 'She needs new clothes. Please take this.'

He pushed a gold coin into Silas's hand. Then he hurried away after Doctor Kimble.

'I don't know that woman,' he told him. 'I thought I did. The child's pretty, isn't she? Marner wants to keep her.'

'I can understand that,' the doctor said. 'I wanted a child too. But let's hurry back to the dance. Your feet are wet and I'm cold.'

They continued walking without speaking. 'I'm sad that she's dead. But I hated Molly,' Godfrey thought. 'Nobody will know my secret now. Dunsey will want to talk if he comes back. But I can give him money and he'll keep quiet.' He could marry Nancy without fear and his future seemed happier. 'I won't tell Nancy about Molly,' he said to himself. 'It will only make us both unhappy. There's my child, of course. But Marner will keep her. She'll stay in the village. I'll give her what she needs. Nobody will know. She'll be happy enough.'

CHAPTER 12

A Child's Love

'You're very kind,' Silas said. 'But I also want to do things for her.
I want her to like me. I can learn.'

S oon everyone in the village was talking about Silas again. 'He's keeping that child,' they said. 'It's a crazy idea. But he's quite a kind old man, after all.' The women were most pleased. Different mothers gave him different information about looking after the child. But they were all worried about the time that a two-year-old child needs. 'He's alone and he has to work. How can he do it?' they asked themselves.

Silas liked Dolly Winthrop best of all the women. He showed her Godfrey's money, and asked her about clothes.

'Oh, Master Marner, don't buy clothes, except a pair of shoes. I've got Aaron's baby clothes. She can have those. She'll grow so fast, and she doesn't really need new things. Aaron's are fine.'

While Dolly found the clothes, Silas heated water. Then Dolly held the child on her knees and washed her. The child laughed and held her toes. Sometimes she made baby noises and called for her mother. But she was not unhappy. Even when her mother was with her, she did not often answer her daughter.

Dolly kissed the clean, golden hair. 'She's prettier than a flower!' she cried. 'And the poor mother died from the cold! That's so sad for the child. But God looked after her. Your door was open and she walked in like a hungry little bird. You were right to keep her, Master Marner. She came to you specially. Not everyone agrees, but I think so. She'll give you some trouble, while she's so small. But I'll come and look after her. I get up early, so I've got a lot of time. I'll be happy to come at about ten o'clock.'

'Thank you – you're very kind,' Silas said. 'But I also want to do things for her. I want her to like me. I can learn.'

'Of course you can,' said Dolly kindly. 'Some men know exactly what children need.' Dolly picked up a little shirt. 'You see this,' she continued. 'You put this on first.'

'Yes,' said Silas. He watched closely. His face was near the child's and she put her arms around his neck. She made baby noises and kissed him.

'You see!' Dolly said. 'She likes you best. She wants to sit on your knee. Take her and put the other clothes on her.'

Silas took the child and her touch woke strange and exciting feelings in him. He took the clothes from Dolly and put them on the child. Dolly told him what to do. The child laughed and played.

'That's good,' Dolly said. 'It's not so difficult, is it?' She watched him, and then asked: 'What will you do with her when you're working? She's a dear little thing but she'll be more trouble every day. She can't reach the fire, but she'll break things. If she can cut herself, she will. I know children.'

Silas thought hard. 'I'll tie her to my loom,' he said. 'I'll tie her with a long piece of cloth.'

'Perhaps that will work. I'll bring her a few toys and she can sit and play with them. I'm sometimes almost sorry that all my children are boys. Girls like to help in the house and wash and make clothes. I can't teach my boys those things. But perhaps one day I can teach this little one.'

'But she'll belong to me,' said Silas quickly.

'Of course she'll be yours, if you're kind to her,' Dolly agreed. 'But you have to be a good father to her. You should take her to church so she can learn with the other children. Then, if she wants God's help, she'll know the right words. My Aaron can say them; the Rector can't say them better.'

Dolly's words troubled Silas. He did not like her talk of God, so he did not answer.

'And there's another thing,' she continued. 'You need to choose a name for the child. What shall we call her?'

'My sister's name was Eppie,' Silas said. 'It's short for Hephzibah.'

'Oh, I like Eppie much better. It's easier and shorter. I'll go now, Master Marner. Don't worry about the dirty clothes. I'll wash them. Ah, isn't she pretty? I'll bring my Aaron and he can show her his toys.'

So, one day, a very clean Silas took Eppie to church. The Rector gave Eppie her new name and welcomed her to the church. Everything was strange to Silas, but he remembered Dolly's words about the child's need for the church. So he took Eppie there every Sunday and met more people from the village.

He had a new interest in his life now. When he had gold, he only wanted to live alone. He could not forget the past. Eppie turned his thoughts to new things and to the future. He took an interest in other families, and thought, 'She, too, will understand a father's love one day.'

In the past, he worked all the time to earn his gold. His eyes saw nothing except the cloth that he was weaving. His ears heard nothing except the noise of his loom. Now Eppie called him away from work. She made every day a holiday. Her fresh young life woke something in his own heart. He saw the signs of spring. Because she was happy, he was happy too.

When summer came, Silas and Eppie enjoyed themselves together. Every day, he carried her past the quarry. He sat in a favourite place and she played. The field was thick with flowers. She picked some and brought them to Silas. Then she listened to the birds. She taught him a game. A bird called; he held up his hand and they both waited. When it called again, he dropped his hand. This was a fine joke, and she laughed and laughed.

Soon she could talk a little and she was always asking questions. Her eyes missed nothing. Then, when she was three years old, there was a problem. She

started behaving badly, like other small children. She did not listen when Silas told her things. This gave him a lot of trouble.

'Just hit her softly, Master Marner,' said Dolly. 'A child needs that sometimes. Or there's another way. You burn wood on your fire. Then put her – just once – in the cupboard where you keep the wood. I did that to Aaron. He's my youngest and I never wanted to hit him. I took him out after a minute, but that was enough. He was dirty and frightened. I washed him and changed his clothes. It was as good as hitting him. But you'll have to choose one way or the other, Master Marner. It's your duty. You must hit her softly, or you must put her in the cupboard. If you don't, she'll never learn to behave.'

Silas was sad. 'She's right,' he thought, 'But I *can't* do it. I can't hurt Eppie. I can't even shake her. If I'm angry with her, perhaps she will love me less.'

As a result of Silas's fear, Eppie saw the possibility for more exciting adventures. One day, Silas was starting a new piece of work. He was using a pair of **scissors** to cut cotton. He usually kept them away from the child, and the sound of the scissors interested her. She watched when he used them. She made plans.

When he stopped using the scissors, Silas sat down. The noise of the loom began. Eppie was sitting on her little bed. She could not go very far because she was tied to the loom with a piece of cloth. But the scissors were not in their usual place. She could reach them.

Very quickly, she left her place and took the scissors. She went back to the bed and turned her back. With little difficulty, she cut the piece of cloth. The door was open. She ran out in the sun. Poor Silas saw nothing. He only thought: 'She is being very good! Very quiet!'

A little later, he needed the scissors. Then he saw that Eppie was not in the room. Frightened, he ran outside. He called her name. His eyes turned towards the red water of the quarry. He was as cold as ice, and his body was shaking. When did she leave the house?

Perhaps she was in one of the fields. She knew the way. The grass was high, and poor Silas searched one field with no result. He went across to the next field. Here, there was a big pool. In winter it was full of water. In summer it was half empty and the sides were soft earth. Eppie sat next to it.

Near her was the deep footprint of an animal. She was using her shoe to fill it with water. She was talking to the shoe in a happy voice. The foot without the shoe was on the wet earth. A sheep was watching her with surprise and fear.

Eppie needed a lesson; that was clear. But Silas could not hit her. He was too happy that she was safe. He picked her up and covered her face with kisses. At the same time, he was almost crying.

scissors /ˈsɪzəz/ (n pl) a tool with two sharp parts for cutting paper and cloth

But when he reached home again, he remembered Dolly's words. 'Perhaps she'll run away again,' he thought. 'And she won't be so lucky a second time. There are so many dangers around. I've got to do something. I don't want to, but I'll put her in the cupboard with the wood.'

The child was on his knees. Suddenly he showed her her dirty feet and clothes, and said: 'Bad Eppie! Eppie is a very bad girl. Eppie took the scissors and cut with them. Then she ran away. Bad girls go into the dark cupboard. Eppie is going to go into the cupboard.'

He waited. 'Perhaps she'll cry and that'll be enough,' he thought. But the idea of a new place excited Eppie. She looked pleased, and began to climb off his knees. There was no other way. He had to do his duty. He was afraid, but he put her into the cupboard. Then he closed the door. Soon a little cry came out: 'Open, open!' Silas opened the door. 'Now Eppie will never be bad again,' he said. 'Or she will go into the cupboard – a bad, black place.'

Silas did not do much work that morning. 'I've done the right thing,' he thought. 'She won't give any more trouble now. But why didn't she cry more?'

In half an hour she was clean again, and she was wearing clean clothes. He turned away from her and saw the long piece of cloth. 'I'll have to mend that,' he said to himself. 'But there's no hurry. She won't give any more trouble now. I'll put her in her little chair near the loom.'

When he next turned round, her face and hands were dirty again. She was looking at him from the cupboard with a sweet smile. 'Eppie's in the cupboard!' she said.

'It's no good,' Silas told Dolly later. 'It's only fun to her. And it will always be the same if I don't hurt her. And I can't do that. If she makes a bit of trouble, I'll live with it.'

So Eppie received only love and smiles from Silas. In the outside world, it was the same. She usually went with him to even the furthest farms. He carried her and his heavy bag of cloth. It was not easy, but he did not want to leave her with Dolly. Everyone in these farms and in the village showed great interest in the weaver's child. They liked him more. In the old days, they were afraid of him. Sometimes they gave him presents, it is true. But that was because he was the only weaver in the area. Now he was one of them; he had a child. They met him with smiles. They invited him into their houses. They asked all the usual questions about young children. Some joked with him: 'You chose a difficult job, Master Marner. Most men leave the little ones to the women. But you weavers have quicker hands than ours, and you understand women's work.'

The older men and women explained all the possible difficulties and dangers. They felt Eppie's round arms and legs. 'Yes, she is well now,' they said. 'But there are so many possible problems. Perhaps you'll be lucky. It'll be a fine thing if she can help you later. Because you'll be old, Master Marner, and you'll need help.'

People often carried Eppie around their farms. Sometimes they showed her the young animals; sometimes they picked fruit from the trees. Other children welcomed her too. And they did not fear Silas when she was near him. He and she were like one person; there was love between them. And there was love between the child and the world. Everybody and everything loved her. So nobody, young or old, feared or hated Silas.

5.1 Were you right?

Look back at Activity 4.4 and then read these sentences. Are they right (✓) or wrong (✗)?

1 ☐ At the New Year's party, Godfrey asks Nancy to marry him.

2 ☐ Godfrey's wife wants his family to see their daughter.

3 ☐ Molly takes the child into Silas's house.

4 ☐ Silas sees Eppie's hair and thinks of his gold.

5 ☐ Silas does not want the child in his house.

6 ☐ Silas tells the Squire and his guests that he has found a dead or dying woman.

7 ☐ Godfrey knows that the child is his.

8 ☐ Godfrey hopes that Molly is dead.

5.2 What more did you learn?

Put a (✓) next to the correct picture.

1 What does Silas do with Eppie while he works?

 A ☐

 B ☐

2 Where does Dolly want Silas to take Eppie?

 A ☐ B ☐

3 Where does Dolly want Silas to put Eppie when she behaves badly?

 A ☐

 B ☐

5.3 Language in use

Look at the sentence in the box. Then find the endings of the sentences below. Write the letters, a–f.

> She felt **that** she had to catch the beautiful light.

1 ☐ Molly often forgets that

2 ☐ Silas knows without a second look that

3 ☐ He sees that

4 ☐ Godfrey hopes that

5 ☐ Mrs Winthrop knows that

6 ☐ Silas understands that

a it is a body under the tree.

b the child looks like his sister.

c Eppie should go to church.

d she has a child.

e Silas needs help with Eppie.

f he can marry Nancy.

5.4 What happens next?

The story continues sixteen years later. Discuss how you think these people's lives have changed. Then make notes.

Notes

Squire Cass:

Godfrey:

Silas:

A Quiet Life

*She learnt from Silas about her mother's death in the snow;
she also knew that Silas was not her father.*

S ixteen years later, it is a bright autumn Sunday in Raveloe. The villagers are
leaving the church. We know a few of them.

That tall, fair man of forty is not very different from the young Godfrey
Cass. The old Squire is dead now, so Godfrey is the new Squire Cass. His eyes
are shining and there are no lines on his face. Perhaps his pretty wife is looking
a bit older. But her strong, kind mouth and clear, honest eyes show that she has
done her duty.

And who is leaving the church after them? Silas Marner's large, brown eyes
see further now and he has more interest in the world around him. But he is
fifty-five and the shape of his back and his white hair give him the look of an old
man. Next to him walks a beautiful girl of eighteen.

A fine young man in a new suit walks behind her. She is the only subject of
his thoughts, and she knows this. But she hides her own thoughts and talks to
her father.

'That's a pretty tree, Father,' Eppie said. 'Perhaps *we* can have a garden. But you can't do it and I don't want you to. It's hard work.'

'Yes, I can,' said Silas. 'The evenings are long and I can do a bit then.'

The path was wider here and the young man came to Eppie's side.

'I can do it for you, Master Marner,' he said. 'I shall enjoy doing it after work.'

'Hello, Aaron.' Silas smiled. 'I didn't see you. If you can help me, we'll soon have a garden.'

'I'll come to the quarry this afternoon,' Aaron told him. 'We can talk about the garden then.'

'You see, Father?' Eppie said. 'You needn't do any hard work. We'll put the plants in after Aaron prepares the ground.'

'That's right,' Aaron said. 'And I can bring you some plants.'

'Thank you,' Silas said. 'You're like your mother – you're very kind.'

'Oh, no,' said Aaron. 'I'm happy to do it. You'll soon have a fine garden. But I should get home now or Mother will miss me. I'll see you this afternoon.' He turned back towards the village and Eppie and Silas continued up the quiet path.

'Oh, Father!' Eppie held Silas's arm tight and kissed him. 'I'm so pleased. I'll really enjoy a little garden.'

'Will you?' said Silas with a quiet smile. 'It'll be a lot of trouble for Aaron.'

Eppie laughed. 'No, it won't,' she said. 'He'll enjoy it.'

When they were near the house, a brown dog ran out. It danced round them. Inside, a cat sat in the sun by the window.

This happy animal life was one new thing about the house, and there were other changes too. Everything was clean and light and showed signs of Dolly Winthrop's help. The fine table and chairs, beds and other furniture came from the old Squire's house. Mr Godfrey Cass was very kind to the weaver. Everyone agreed about that.

Silas sat down and watched Eppie. She covered the table with a clean cloth and took the hot food from the fireplace. Silas loved his stone fireplace. It was a true friend, like the old brown pot. Most important of all, it was where he found Eppie.

He ate quietly, and soon put down his knife and fork. He watched Eppie. The cat was climbing up her arm and she was laughing. Her golden hair and white neck shone against the dark blue colour of her dress. The dog and the cat were on each side of her. She held up a piece of food and they both wanted it. Then she broke it in two and gave a piece to each of them.

'If you're ready, Father,' Eppie said, 'go outside. It's a beautiful day. Sit in the sun and smoke.'

Outside, many thoughts filled his head. Years ago he was a very unhappy man. Now he accepted the Raveloe way of life and the village people accepted him. He thought about William Dane and Lantern Yard. He was happy there too. He remembered talking to Dolly about that time and asking her about it. 'Why did that dark shadow cover the best years of my life?' he asked her.

'I don't know,' Dolly told him. 'You stopped believing in God. Perhaps if a man doesn't believe in God, he can't be happy. Without God, he is without any other friends. A man has to believe and to help other people.'

'But I couldn't believe when I left Lantern Yard,' he told her. 'It was too difficult.'

'Of course it was,' Dolly agreed. 'I can talk, but I wasn't in your place. I'm sorry.'

'No, no,' said Silas. 'You're right. There's good in this world. I can feel it now. But we don't always see it. A lot of good is hidden behind our problems and the bad times. William Dane hurt me badly, but then the child came to my house. Things like that are not accidents.'

This discussion took place when Eppie was quite small. Now she was becoming a woman. Because their love was complete, Silas always told her everything. And because village people are always talking, no other way was possible. Everyone knew about Eppie's arrival in the village. So she learnt from Silas about her mother's death in the snow; she also knew that Silas was not her father.

When she grew older, Silas gave her her mother's ring. Her thoughts were of her mother, and she did not ask about her real father. She knew the happiness of a mother's love; Mrs Winthrop was an excellent example. Again and again, she asked Silas questions about her mother. What kind of person was she? What did she look like? How did he find her under the tree?

On this afternoon, Eppie looked at the little tree when she came out of the house. 'Father,' she said. Her voice was soft and sad. 'Let's move the tree to the garden. It can go in a corner and I'll put flowers round it.'

'We won't forget the tree,' Silas promised. 'But we need a wall around the garden. If we don't have one, animals will come in. They'll eat the plants.'

'There are a lot of stones,' Eppie said. 'We'll use those. Look there! They're all around the quarry.' She walked to the quarry to show him. Then she gave a little cry of surprise. 'Father! Come and look. The water's gone down. Yesterday the quarry was quite full.'

Silas came to her side and explained. 'They were working on Mr Cass's fields around here. They decided that these fields hold too much water. So they cut narrow paths across the fields and now the water can run away. Our land will be drier too.'

'Oh! It's too heavy!' Eppie tried to carry a stone, but dropped it.

'Come and sit down,' Silas told her. 'You need someone's help – and my arms aren't strong enough now.'

They sat quietly together and Eppie held her father's hand. Shadows from a tree danced around them.

'Father,' Eppie said at last. 'If I marry, shall I wear my mother's wedding ring?'

Silas turned to look at her. 'Does Aaron want to marry you?'

'Yes. He's almost twenty-four and he's got a lot of work.'

'Will you accept him?'

'I think so. But I shan't leave you. Aaron wants us all to live together. He says that he'll be as good as a son to you.'

'Aren't you too young?'

'I don't know. I'm very happy with you. I don't want any change.'

Silas thought for a minute and then he said, 'Things will change, Eppie. I'll get older and need more help. I know that you'll be happy to help me. But it's not right. I want you to have a husband. Someone young and strong – someone who will look after you until the end of your life.' He thought again. 'I like Aaron,' he said. 'I like him very much. I know that you do too. We'll ask Mrs Winthrop. She always knows what's best.'

'Look!' said Eppie. Dolly and Aaron were coming along the path to Silas's house. 'There they are.'

'We'll go and meet them.' Silas stood up and helped Eppie to her feet.

CHAPTER 14

Trouble in Raveloe

'I didn't tell her my secret when I first married her. I can't tell her now;
I don't want to destroy our love.'

O n that same afternoon, Nancy Cass was sitting alone. Godfrey was out. 'I'm going to the fields by the quarry,' her husband told her before he left. 'I want to look at the work there. The fields will probably be dry now. I'll be back at teatime.'

Nancy thought about Godfrey. He was quiet and kind, but there was often a sad look in his eyes. 'Is it because we haven't got any children?' she asked herself. 'A woman can spend all her time looking after her husband. But a man wants to plan for his family. A man needs a wife – and children too. Godfrey wanted to **adopt** a child. Was I wrong to refuse?'

Nancy did not think that the adoption of other people's children was a good idea. She and Godfrey talked about it many times after the early death of Nancy's baby. They were both very sad about the death. 'We should adopt a child,' Godfrey said at that time. 'It will make our lives happier.'

But Nancy did not want an adopted child. The years passed and they were unable to have more children. But she continued to refuse. 'It's not right,' she

adopt /əˈdɒpt/ (v) to take a child into your family and make that child legally your son or daughter

said. 'Don't you remember that lady in Royston? She adopted a child and it behaved very badly. I can't agree, dear. If we have no children, that's hard. But it's for God to decide.'

'Why should a child bring trouble on us?' Godfrey said. 'Marner adopted a child. They're happier together than most people. But he's a poor man. It's difficult for him to look after the girl. We can adopt Eppie.'

Godfrey never told Nancy about his first wife, Molly. He was sad that they had no children. But most of all he wanted Eppie, his own child, and he could not explain the reason to Nancy. He did not think about Silas. Silas loved Eppie more than life itself, but Godfrey did not understand this. 'Marner will want the best for Eppie,' he thought. 'He needn't worry about money. Money is a problem for him and I can solve it.'

But Nancy did not agree to this either. 'God decides these matters, dear,' she told him. 'He knows better than we do. If we adopt a child, we'll be sorry.'

So Godfrey did not talk about Eppie again. He understood his wife's feelings. In some matters, she was the stronger person. Sometimes, because of this, he was a little afraid of her.

'I can never tell her about my first wife,' he thought. 'If I do, perhaps she'll hate the child. I didn't tell her my secret when I first married her. I can't tell her now; I don't want to destroy our love.'

So Nancy was thinking about Godfrey. 'Was I wrong?' she asked herself. 'Old people feel the need for children. If I die, Godfrey will be alone. But I can't look into the future. I'll just do my best now.'

A girl came in with the tea. Nancy looked at her and asked, 'Has the master come back, Jane?'

'No,' Jane said. She was excited about something. 'Can you see all the people? They're hurrying past the front window. Perhaps there's been an accident.'

'Oh, it won't be anything bad,' said Nancy. 'Perhaps one of Mr Snell's animals has got out again.'

'Even farm animals sometimes attack people,' said Jane. She was frightened, but she was enjoying her fear.

When Jane left, Nancy got up. She went to the front window. 'That girl is always putting fears into my head,' she said to herself. 'When *will* Godfrey come?' She could see nothing along the road. 'I'm worrying like a child,' she thought. 'There's no sign of trouble. Why am I afraid? Godfrey won't return this way; he'll come across the fields.'

But she continued to stand there. She looked at the church, and at the trees in the Rector's garden. The beautiful view did not take away her fear. The fear grew. A shadow is darker on a bright day.

CHAPTER 15

Secrets

*He did not move or look at her. She waited. 'He hasn't finished,'
she thought. 'There's more to tell.'*

G odfrey opened the door. Nancy turned from the window with happy eyes. 'Dear, you've come at last! I'm so happy. I–'

She stopped suddenly. Godfrey was putting down his hat. His hand was shaking and his face was white. He sat down like an old man and said quietly, 'Please sit down, my dear. I've got some terrible news.'

'It isn't – Father?' Nancy asked. Her voice shook as she sat down.

'No,' Godfrey said. 'It's Dunstan. He left sixteen years ago and he never returned. Now they've found his body. There isn't much of it.' He put his hand to his head. Nancy waited and then he continued: 'The quarry is dry now. The water has gone after our work in the fields. He's down there. There's his watch and his ring. And there's my riding stick with the gold top. After sixteen years, there he lies between two great stones.'

Godfrey stopped again.

'What's wrong?' Nancy cried. 'Is there something worse to tell? Did he kill himself?'

'No, he didn't kill himself,' Godfrey said quietly. 'But there is something worse. He was the thief. Dunstan took Silas Marner's gold.'

'Oh, Godfrey!' Nancy cried. She felt very sorry for her husband. He did not move or look at her. She waited. 'He hasn't finished,' she thought. 'There's more to tell.'

At last he continued: 'There are no secrets in the end, Nancy. I've got a secret that I can't hide from you now. I don't want others to tell you and I don't want to die first. So I'll tell you.'

Nancy looked at him in fear. Their eyes met. Each was like a stranger to the other.

'When I married you, I behaved very badly,' he told her. 'I hid something from you. You remember Eppie's mother? Marner found her dead in the snow outside his house. That woman was my wife. Eppie is my child.'

Nancy looked quickly away from him. 'You'll never feel the same about me again,' Godfrey said, and his voice shook a little. Nancy did not answer.

'I hid it all from you,' he continued sadly. 'I failed in my duty to the child. But I loved you so much and I didn't want you to refuse me. I didn't love my first wife. She was a bad woman. It was a terrible time.'

He waited in great fear. Finally, Nancy lifted her eyes to his and spoke. Her voice was not angry – only very sad.

'Why didn't you tell me this when you first wanted Eppie here? I refused because I didn't know everything. I could never refuse *your* child.' She began to cry. 'Oh, Godfrey, why didn't you bring her to our house from the start? We had the possibility of a happy life together. When my little baby died, I–' She could say nothing more.

'I couldn't tell you. I wanted your love. Could you love me in those days with a child?' he asked.

'I can't tell. I never wanted to marry another man. But you were wrong to hide all this. It's wrong to live a lie.'

'Can you ever forgive me?' he asked.

'You haven't hurt me, Godfrey. You're a good husband to me. But you should do the right thing for Eppie.'

'We can take her now. I shan't hide things any more.'

'It will be different,' said Nancy in a sad voice. 'She's not a child now. But you should accept her as yours and bring her here to live with us. I'll do my duty to her too. Perhaps, with God's help, she will love me.'

6.1 Were you right?

1 Look back at Activity 5.4. Then write answers to these questions.

  a How old are Silas and Eppie now?   ....

  b Who wants to marry Eppie?   ....

  c Does Silas want Eppie to marry him?   ....

  d Who has refused to adopt a child?   ....

  e What does Godfrey fear?   ....

  f Who and what are found in the quarry?   ....

2 What is this? Why is it so important in Silas's life?

....

....

....

....

....

....

....

....

6.2 What more did you learn?

Put these sentences in the correct order, from 1–8.

a ☐ Godfrey tells Nancy that Dunstan stole Silas's gold.

b ☐ Nancy suggests that Eppie should live with her and Godfrey now.

c ☐ Nancy and Godfrey had a baby but it died.

d ☐ Godfrey tells his wife that he has failed in his duty to his child.

e ☐ Godfrey tells Nancy that Dunstan's body is in the quarry.

f ☐ Eppie asks Silas about her mother's wedding ring.

g ☐ Eppie discovers that the water has gone down in the quarry.

h ☐ Nancy learns from her husband that Eppie is his child.

6.3 Language in use

Read the sentences in the box. Then write *should, shouldn't, shall* or *shan't* in the sentences below.

> 'I **should** get home now or Mother will miss me.'
>
> 'I **shall** enjoy doing it after work.'

1 'I .... hide the truth from you now,' Godfrey said decisively.

   'I .... tell you everything.'

2 'I .... do the right thing for Eppie. I .... ask her to live with us. Do you agree that that's right?'

3 'I .... live a lie. I know it's wrong. And I .... hope for your forgiveness.'

6.4 What happens next?

1 What do you think Eppie will say to Godfrey when he tells her everything? Write two or three sentences.

....

....

....

2 Discuss how the story will end for these people.

CHAPTER 16

Father and Daughter

'Why don't you take the heart out of my body? God gave her to me when you didn't want her.'

Silas and Eppie were sitting together at home. On the table near them lay the gold.

'I counted it every night,' Silas said. 'When it was stolen, my life was completely empty. I wanted to have it back and feel it again. Then you came. Your old father felt so much for you! You didn't know then, Eppie, when you were small.'

'But I know now.' Eppie took his hand. 'You saved me from a life in a children's home. A child gets no love there.'

'My dear, you saved me from a future that was far worse. My troubles almost killed me. The money was stolen at the right time. Now it's back again at the right time, because you'll need it for your marriage.'

They heard visitors outside the door. Eppie opened it and welcomed Mr and Mrs Godfrey Cass in her polite, country way.

'I'm sorry that it's so late,' Nancy said. She looked pale and worried. Eppie put out two chairs and stood next to Silas.

Godfrey was frightened too, but he hid his fear. 'I'm pleased about the money, Marner,' he said. 'My family hurt you. I'm very sorry and I want to repay you for your trouble. I have behaved badly too – it's not just my brother, Marner.'

Silas looked at him in surprise. 'Sir, you've helped us in many ways,' he said. 'The money wasn't your fault – and it's here now.'

'*You* can look at it in that way, Marner, but *I* can't,' Godfrey told him. 'You worked hard for that money.'

'Oh, sir,' Silas smiled. 'Work was my only friend in my time of trouble.'

Godfrey did not understand. He was thinking his own thoughts, and continued: 'Yes, you worked hard – and you need a rest. You're not a young man. We're all growing old and that money on the table isn't very much. It won't last for ever. Remember – there are two of you!'

'Even when I'm old, Eppie and I will be happy enough, sir,' Silas said quietly. 'We don't want much. Not many men like me save so much. Perhaps the money's nothing to someone like you, sir. But it's a lot to us.'

Godfrey was not pleased with himself. He was not explaining his business well. The difficulty of it surprised him.

'You should plan for your future,' he said quietly. 'You want Eppie to enjoy life, don't you? She's not as strong as the other village girls, and a hard life and hard work will be bad for her. If a rich family takes her, she won't have to work hard. They can turn her into a lady and leave her their money.'

A sudden fear shook Silas. 'What do you mean, sir?' he asked.

'Mrs Cass and I have no children,' Godfrey explained slowly. 'We have a good home and more than enough money. But we are the only ones who enjoy them. We want to have somebody in place of a daughter. We want to have Eppie as our own child. After all this time, you'll be pleased, won't you? Eppie, of course, will always love and remember you. She'll come and see you very often. We'll help you in every possible way.'

Eppie put her hand on Silas's shoulder. At first he could not speak, but then he said, 'Eppie, my dear, I won't keep you if you want to go.'

Eppie felt her father's deep unhappiness. She thanked the Casses politely and then she said, 'I can't leave my father. Nobody can be closer to me. Thank you again, but I can't be a lady. I can't leave my friends.'

Her voice shook a little. With a cry, Silas put his hand on hers. Nancy's eyes were full of tears. She was sorry for Eppie, and for Godfrey too, but she said nothing.

Eppie's words were a complete surprise to Godfrey. After all these years, he was behaving well. Why couldn't Eppie and Silas understand that? When he spoke again, he sounded angry.

'I have the strongest of all reasons for my suggestion, Eppie,' he said slowly. He turned to Silas. 'Marner – Eppie is my child and I need to look after her. It's my duty, and not the duty of another man. She's my own child. Her mother was my wife.'

When Eppie cried out, it freed Silas from his fear. He knew that she did not want to leave him. The thought made him stronger and some of his old hate came back. 'Why didn't you tell me sixteen years ago?' he said in a cold, hard voice. 'I didn't love her then. Why do you want to take her now? Why don't you take the heart out of my body? God gave her to me when you didn't want her. I took her into my home, and in God's eyes she's my child. She isn't yours because you never accepted her.'

'I know. I was wrong. I'm very sorry,' Godfrey said quietly.

'Those sixteen years don't change because you're sorry now. You call yourself her father. She called me Father as soon as she could say the word. And she does to this day.'

'I've said I'm sorry.' Godfrey spoke more loudly. 'Listen to me, Marner. Think about it. She's not going out of your life. She'll be very near and she'll visit you very often. She'll feel the same towards you.'

'Oh, will she?' said Silas in an even angrier voice. 'How will she feel the same? Every day, we eat the same food and drink the same drink. We have the same thoughts. She'll feel the same? That's empty talk.'

'You love Eppie, Marner,' Godfrey said angrily. 'Don't you want a happy life for her? Or is your own enjoyment more important to you? Remember your age, and hers. Time is short. Perhaps she'll marry a village boy. Then her possibility of a good home and my money will end. You're taking that away from her. I don't want to hurt you – you did so much, and I did nothing – but I have to look after my own daughter. It's my duty.'

These words woke deep memories in Eppie. She turned her thoughts from her old, much-loved father towards this new, strange father. When she was a baby, he was only a shadow. This shadow had put a wedding ring on her mother's finger. But here was the real man. Her thoughts went back to his life with her mother. They turned then to a possible life with him in the future. She did not want this life. She did not like him as a father. But she did not decide for this reason. She decided because she loved Silas.

Silas was frightened of losing her. But nothing mattered to Silas except Eppie's happiness. After a long time he spoke, and his voice shook. 'I'll say no more. Have your own way. Speak to the child. I won't stop you.'

Godfrey looked at his daughter. She was not a child now. He was afraid that she hated him.

'Eppie, my dear,' he said, 'Marner was a good father to you. We'll always want you to show him your love and thanks. We'll always give you our help in this. But we, too, are asking for your love. I was not a good father. I know that. The rest of my life will be different. I want to please you in every way. As my only child, you'll have everything. And my wife will be the best of mothers. After all these years, you'll have a mother's love again.'

'My dear, you'll be everything to me,' said Nancy in her soft voice. 'Our life will be complete with our daughter.'

Eppie did not move. She kept her hand on Silas's shoulder, and spoke in a strong, cold voice. She thanked them both again for their offers.

'You are very kind, sir, and your suggestion is too much for me. I shall never be happy again if I leave my father alone here. We are happy together every day of our lives. I can't enjoy anything without him. He had nobody before I came. What will he have if I go now? From the start, he looked after me and loved me. I'll stay with him for ever. Nobody will ever come between him and me.'

Nancy looked at Godfrey. But he was looking down at the floor. His thoughts were far away. She was his wife. She had to help him.

'My dear,' she said, 'I understand. Of course you want to stay here. But you have a duty to your real father. He is offering you his home. Will it be right if you refuse him?'

'In my heart, I know only one father,' said Eppie. Her eyes were wet with tears. 'He'll sit in a corner of our little home and I shall do everything for him. I don't want any other home. I can't live like a lady. I like poor people and their houses and their ways. And I'm going to marry a poor man. I've promised. He'll live here, and together we shall look after Father.'

So Godfrey's plan failed. Eppie did not want his love. It was too late. This was the result of his worst actions. His face was red and his eyes hurt. Suddenly, he felt a great need for air.

'We should go,' he said in a low voice, and without another word he left the room.

Nancy got up. 'We won't talk more now. We want the best for you, my dear – and for you too, Marner. We shall come and see you again. It's late now.'

She said goodbye and left them.

CHAPTER 17

Husband and Wife

He put out his hand. Nancy took it, and he pulled her towards him.
'That's the end of that,' he said.

G odfrey did not speak on the way home. After their return, he sat down in his favourite chair. Nancy stood near him and waited. At last Godfrey turned his head towards her. Each of them looked at the other. They did not need words.

After a time he put out his hand. Nancy took it, and he pulled her towards him.

'That's the end of that,' he said.

She kissed him. 'Yes,' she said. 'We can't continue with your plan, can we? She doesn't want to be our daughter, and we can't change her mind.'

'No,' Godfrey agreed. 'Some duties are different from others. If you borrow money, you can pay it back at any time. You pay a little more, that's all. But other duties won't wait. It's too late now. Marner was right. If a man refuses a good thing, another man will have it. I didn't want people to know about my child at that time. Now I do, but it has to stay a secret.'

'So you won't tell people about you and Eppie?' Nancy asked after a minute or two.

'No. What good will it do? She has chosen her own life, and I'll help her in every possible way. She wants to marry someone, doesn't she? I need to know his name.'

'We won't worry Father and Priscilla, then,' said Nancy. 'We'll only tell them about Dunsey. We should do that, of course.'

'I'll put the facts in a letter, perhaps,' said Godfrey. 'People found out about Dunsey by accident – I don't want them to find out about me in the same way. At the end of my life, they can open the letter and learn the truth. But I don't want to tell anyone now. Eppie can be happy in her own way. Oh, I remember now – doesn't she want to marry Aaron Winthrop? I saw him with her and Marner at the church.'

'He's a good young man, and he works hard,' said Nancy. She wanted to make her husband feel better.

After a time Godfrey said in a sad voice, 'She's a very nice, pretty girl, isn't she, Nancy?'

'Yes, dear – and she has your hair and eyes. I didn't see that before, but it's very clear to me now.'

'But she doesn't like me, does she? Not now. She liked me before. But she changed when I told her the truth. '

'Marner is a father to her. She didn't like the idea of change.'

'No, she doesn't like me. I behaved badly towards her, but that isn't the only reason. She thinks that her mother's death is my fault. And I'll have to accept that. I can never tell her about that woman's life. It *is* my fault. I was crazy when I married her. I behaved badly towards you. And then I behaved badly towards the child.'

Nancy said nothing. He was right, and she did not want to help him with a lie. After a minute or two, he continued in a softer voice, 'But I've got *you*, Nancy. And I'm very lucky; nothing matters except that.'

'You are always good to me, Godfrey. Just accept what God decides. Then I shall be completely happy.'

'I'll try to accept it, my dear. It's not too late. But I can't change the past. It *is* too late for that.'

CHAPTER 18

New Beginnings

*Four very happy people walked through the gate and
the flowers welcomed them.*

I n Raveloe, weddings were usually in the spring. It was the best time, because
all the plants were starting to flower. People were not too busy on the farms
and the weather was not too cold.

The sun was very warm on Eppie's wedding day. This was lucky, because her
wedding dress was a very light one. Eppie could not pay for it herself. But she
chose it and Mrs Godfrey Cass bought it for her. It was made of white cotton
with a few small pink flowers on it.

Before the wedding she said to her father, 'I'm not leaving you, Father. There
won't be any changes and you'll have Aaron as your son.'

After the wedding, she walked from the church through the village. One
hand was on her husband's arm and the other held her father's hand. Her white
dress and golden hair shone in the sun. Dolly Winthrop was with them.

Miss Priscilla Lammeter, Nancy's sister, and her father drove past. They watched with enjoyment; everyone loves a wedding. They were visiting Nancy, because Godfrey was away. He could not go to the wedding, but he was paying for it. 'Of course he feels a great interest in the weaver,' Priscilla thought. 'His own brother stole from the poor man.'

'Why couldn't Nancy have a child like that?' she said to her father. 'Nothing can take the place of a child in a family.'

'Yes, my dear,' said her father. 'One feels that in later life. Old people are young again in the company of children.'

Nancy came out of the church and welcomed her father and sister. The wedding group went on its way until they came to the quarry.

There were many changes to Silas's house and it had a garden now. Godfrey Cass was paying for everything. He even offered Silas and Eppie a new home, but they wanted to stay at the quarry.

The garden was full of flowers. It had a stone wall around it and the gate at the front was open. Four very happy people walked through the gate and the flowers welcomed them.

'Oh, Father,' said Eppie, 'we have a very pretty home! Nobody in the world is happier than we are.'

1 **It is two days after Eppie and Aaron's wedding. Work with another student and have this conversation.**

Student A	You are Silas Marner. You have learnt a lot about gold, thieves, secrets and family life over the years. Tell Aaron about your life. You do not want him to make the mistakes that you and others have made. You want him to be a good husband to Eppie.

Student B	You are Aaron. Listen to Silas's stories and ask questions. You want to do what is right. Promise to be a good husband to Eppie.

2 **Discuss the pictures below.**

a Why are they important to the story of *Silas Marner*? Is there an important picture missing? What is it?

b Imagine that this story is written about people today. What should you change these pictures to?

Imagine that you are a person from the story. Write about your opinion of adoption. How did adoption, or the refusal to adopt, change your life?

Adoption:
For or Against

1 What is most important for a happy life, in your opinion? Number these from 1 (the most important) to 10 (the least important). Then discuss your opinions with two or three other students. Do they agree with you?

Happiness is:

- [ ] money
- [ ] travel and excitement
- [ ] time for private interests
- [ ] family
- [ ] love and marriage
- [ ] parties and fun
- [ ] professional success
- [ ] friends
- [ ] religion
- [ ] good health

2 What do you know about Paul McCartney and Heather Mills's marriage? Talk to the other students in your group and answer these questions.

a Which one has made a lot of money? How did he or she earn it?

....

....

b How long were they married?

....

c What has been written about their marriage in the newspapers?

....

....

d Has money brought them happiness, do you think? Why (not)?

....

....

....

74

3 Money can buy happiness! Use the Internet to find more information about these people. Find out more, too, about a rich person from your country who helps others. Discuss how these four people earned their money. How have they used large amounts of it to help other people?

Bono has helped ....

....

Yusuf Islam (Cat Stevens) has helped ....

....

Oprah Winfrey has helped ....

....

.... has helped ....

....

....

4 Imagine that, as a group, you have just won a very large amount of money. You want to use some of it to help other people. Make a list of five groups of people in the world who need help.

We want to help:

5 Imagine that it is now ten years later. How has your money changed the lives of the people that you helped? Write about it for a magazine. Ask other people to act in the same way.